Flawed Decisions Murder

Mia Tenroc

Flawed Decision Murders by Mia Tenroc
© 2019 Mia Tenroc
ISBN: 978-1-944433-04-8 (paperback)

McToner Publishing Inc.
P.O. Box 37
Goldenrod, Florida 32722
McTonerPublishing@gmail.com
www.miatenroc.com

All rights are reserved. This book, or any portion thereof may not be used or reproduced without written permission by McToner Publishing or the author. Any scanning, uploading, and distributing of this publication without the permission of the publisher is illegal and punishable by law.

This is a work of fiction. Names, characters, places, and incidents either are the product of the author's imagination or used fictitiously. Any resemblance to actual person, living or dead, business establishments, events, or locales is entirely coincidental.

If you purchase this book without a cover, you should be aware that this book is stolen property. It was reported as "unsold and destroyed" to the publisher, and neither the author nor the publisher has received any payment for this "stripped book."

Permission:
ID 121570017 © Sean Pavone / Dreamstime.com – Front and Back Cover Photos
Cover & Formatting by Eric Cornett
Authors photo by Ivy Neville Photography

DEDICATION

This has been the first year of my life that I have seen friend and families split over the current political situation. I wanted to write a book that expressed that sadness of ended relationship.

ACKNOWLEDGMENTS

Last December, the opportunity arose to meet some of the people in Sugarloaf, New York that purchased my books. Thank you so much for your support and encouragement.

Cast of Characters

Group of Friends:

Jean – A murder mystery writer who had involvement with murders in the past and tells the stories of her adventures to her friends. Her partner in life is police detective Nick Noble.

Josephine, aka Jo – Jean's sister, a vegetarian and animal lover who is into gardening and holistic medicine. She is married to Michael.

Francesca Anne, goes by Fannie Annie – Jean's lifelong friend. She is an eccentric bohemian that runs a secondhand shop. She loves to make herself the talk of the town.

Belinda – The optimistic, outgoing one of the group. She retired from a high-power marketing career. She and her family are well connected in high society circles. She is married to Steve.

Priscilla – Jean's next-door neighbor and friend. She is the quiet person of the group that prefers to listen rather than talk. She is close to her daughter and grandsons.

Eve – An accountant that works from home part-time. She lives next door to Josephine. Her husband is Nigel, who lives out in the country and is a hoarder of junk.

Nick Noble – A veteran police detective and Jean's boyfriend. He is always in trouble with his supervisor because of Jean's involvement in many of his cases.

Janice Hoover – Nick's intelligent but hotheaded police partner.

Key people related to the murder in the Spiritual Church:

Bob – A good-looking but egotistical, selfish man. He uses other people, including his own family, solely to make life better for himself.

Lottie – A wealthy, hardworking, good-natured but unattractive woman. She is seeking a husband and currently has her eyes set on Bob.

Helena – The Head Pastor at the church. She is a domineering, spiteful woman who seeks revenge on those who challenge her.

Grace – Helena's mentally-challenged daughter. She's the bookkeeper for the church but has her unique way of keeping the records.

Lisette – The beautiful Assistant Pastor at the church. She sings like an angel and has pure thoughts for all.

Richard – Lisette's husband who notices that Bob has lustful feelings for his wife.

Violet – A Native American member of the church. She prefers to just be an anonymous face in the crowd but gets thrusted into a leadership role due to Bob's meddling.

Key people related to the murder in Abletown:

Missy aka Trudy Mist – A woman of questionable morals that has inserted herself into the mayor race of Abletown.

Peter Cranbert – The Mayor of Abletown for the past 20 years. He is selling out the town to major land developers for personal gain, much to the town's protest.

Leon Pierre – A former mayor of a big city. He dislikes the decisions Peter has made at the town's expense and has decided to run against him.

Billy Grely – A photographer willing to take any type of pictures for the right price.

Gwen – A newcomer to Abletown that has the town in a gossiping frenzy.

Abletown

Chapter 1 – Broom

"Broom! Can you believe someone would choose that word as the license plate for their car? What kind of message are they trying to send?" Eve said in an animated fashion.

Belinda just lifted an eyebrow suggesting with humor, "Maybe she's a witch and believes her car is her method of transportation."

Josephine agreed, "When I saw a new person had moved to the neighborhood, I took over some freshly baked oatmeal and raisin cookies. She opened the door just slightly. I introduced myself and said welcome to the neighborhood and extended the bag to her. All she said was thank you. She didn't tell me her name or invite me in. She took the cookies and closed the door."

FLAWED DECISIONS MURDER

Eve picked up the conversation. "After Josephine told me of her experience, I took over a plant thinking maybe she was unfriendly because she couldn't eat sweets. I received the same treatment."

The weekday morning conversation on the front porch of the Friend's Home was usually about traveling or telling of mysteries. Jean suggested, "If we are going to do town gossip, why don't we go to Fannie Annie's Attic for our tea? I don't want to hear the repeat of this conversation for her benefit later today."

The five friends, Jean, Josephine aka Jo, Belinda, Eve, and Priscilla walked the few blocks to the second-hand store even though it was closed on Monday to the public. Jean wanted her friend, Fannie, to open a tea room when she decided to start a business in Abletown, but Fannie hated tea and refused. Jean decided to keep tea in Fannie's store so the ladies walked over every day and Jean made tea for them.

Fannie, who was hard at work with the inventory when they arrived, turned to greet them. "I was at the diner for breakfast today. The talk around town is the new neighbor on Third Street across from you, Jo and Eve. Have you met her yet?"

The story of the cookies and plant was retold. Jean said, "I believe the problem was the cookies. If you don't come bearing chocolate chip cookies, you should expect a cold shoulder."

MIA TENROC

Josephine rolled her eyes. "I know your feelings on cookies. Would you like me to make some chocolate chip this week?"

Jean smiled and nodded yes. "So glad you got the hint."

Priscilla looked worried. "I'm supposed to take over the 'Welcome to Town' brochures over to her but I can't handle rude people. Maybe I can send someone from the Senior Center staff over with them."

Fannie looked surprised, "I believe everyone I don't know is an opportunity to make a new friend. The less welcoming they are, the more I enjoy the challenge of winning them over. I will be glad to take them over with you, Priscilla. Hey Jean, would you like to join us so you can tell her about water aerobics?"

Jean suggested, "I think two people at one time is enough. Since Priscilla attends the classes, she can extend the offer. I think too many of us might look like an attack of the older ladies' gang."

Belinda spoke. "I'm sure we will know about this lady soon enough but I want to change the subject. I decided to work on the campaign for Leon Pierre. I start this afternoon at the headquarters on Second Street. Do any of you want to join me?"

FLAWED DECISIONS MURDER

Priscilla was noticeably upset. "Peter Cranbert has been our mayor for years. He's a good guy and I don't like change. Why aren't you supporting him?"

Belinda was in authority mode in as she spoke, "It's not that Peter isn't nice but I believe that we need to preserve the historic section of this town by a zoning ordinance. There are builders wanting to tear down some of these lovely mansions to put up condos or turn the existing homes into multi-family units. I'm against the destruction of our town and so is Leon. That is why I'm supporting him."

Priscilla spoke sourly, "If they own the house, they should be able to do what they want with it."

Belinda explained, "I wouldn't want a bunch of modern buildings in this historic town. It's more than just the building. If they left the outside the same, I wouldn't mind as much, but most of the homes have no garages so there would be more people needing to park on the street than we have spaces available. That matter aside, they are talking about adding more families than we can handle right now. There would be a need for more school teachers, more water and sewer services, and more traffic. The houses in town weren't built to handle the extra load. With only about 1,500 people in town, we can't afford the extra expenses. We would need the developers to pay for all that increase in cost. They don't want to and Peter doesn't understand that."

MIA TENROC

Jean added to the conversation. "I talked with Peter's wife. He wants to retire and move to a hunting cabin in the woods. Peter went with Leon to his cabin and hasn't stopped talking about it. She refuses to sell their home in town and they don't have enough money for two houses. Peter is only running for mayor because he said it is a way to earn the money they need. The position doesn't pay that much so I question how he thinks he can earn it. I plan to keep a sharp eye on what happens next."

Fannie said, "Peter came to the store asking for campaign funds. In a town this size, there is minimal expense for a campaign. Most people just go to the diner and talk to the people eating. There are debates at the church or the Senior Center. He promised that if I gave money and he won there would be a lot more people in town to come to my business. I don't know how he can promise that. Jean and Eve, I think you two should investigate the finances of both groups and keep the community advised."

The group departed for water aerobics but you could tell there was a tension between the friends because of the political talk.

Abletown

Chapter 2 – Friendship Fray

The next morning, the ladies gather on the porch. Priscilla still acted odd. Jean asked, "Is there something wrong, Priscilla?"

Like a dam breaking loose, Priscilla unloaded. "You were wrong to tell everyone about the cabin that Peter wants. You shouldn't gossip about something that was probably told in confidence."

Jean stayed calm but was clearly upset herself, "The information about the cabin was told at a meeting at the church. There were 10 people there. I doubt that it was in confidence. If it was told in a private conversation, I wouldn't repeat the story. I'm not that type of person, and I'm offended you think that I would break a confidence."

MIA TENROC

Priscilla realized the hurt her words had caused. "I'm sorry. I didn't realize it was common knowledge. That was wrong of her to say anything to the church friends. She must not have realized the harm she did to her husband's chances in his run for mayor."

Jean took the high road, "I accept your apology. She also said she doesn't want him running for mayor. She wants to retire from public life. Let's change the subject. I've been thinking of all the things that the license plate 'Broom' could mean. Maybe that woman owns a cleaning business. There could be other reasons for the word broom other than being a witch. There are people that like to make old fashion brooms as a hobby or decorate them for a wall hanging. Maybe she or someone she knows is a chimney sweep. It's fun to think of all the things it might mean."

Eve suggested, "I will try to find out what type of church she goes to. If it is a Spiritualist Church, the witch hypothesis might be true."

"Didn't you have to investigate a murder at a Spiritualist Church, Jean?" asked Josephine.

Jean smiled, "I would say investigate is an overstatement. I was a reporter on the criminal division of a newspaper. It was an interesting murder if you want to hear the story."

FLAWED DECISIONS MURDER

It was agreed that the story would be told on the porch for the next few mornings.

Belinda asked Priscilla, "Did you and Fannie go to the witch's house yesterday?"

Priscilla blushed, "I was busy at the Center so Fannie went in my place to deliver the welcome."

Jean said, "I think we should go to see Fannie to see if the witch talked to her. Fannie likes to play 20 questions with anyone she meets. I can't imagine anyone not talking to Fannie."

When they walked in, Fannie shouted, "You just missed Gwen. I would have loved for you to meet her."

"Who's Gwen?" asked Jean.

Fannie looked surprised, "Why the new neighbor that lives across from Jo and Eve, of course."

Eve opened her eyes wide, "She told you her name?"

Fannie laughed, "Of course. We had a nice visit. She lives alone. She used to live in the city but from what I can understand, she and her husband divorced so she moved here. She left with just minimal possessions and she came here to shop today."

Jo asked, "Did you ask about the license plate? Did you ask if she attended church?"

8

MIA TENROC

Fannie knew how curious the others were and loved playing a game with them by not disclosing too much. "No, those two things never came up. The only thing I said was the whole town has noticed her 'Broom' license plate and she should keep it a secret if she wants to stay the talk of the town. Then Gwen just laughed so I don't know."

After the visit, the other ladies headed to the Home to do water aerobics. Belinda said, "I'm going to the Leon headquarters at 2:00 p.m. everyday to work the phones if anyone wants to join me."

Sending an icy glare toward Belinda, Priscilla stated, "I'm going to Peter's headquarters to volunteer my time there."

Belinda ignored the negative reaction and said, "I look forward to seeing everyone on the porch tomorrow for the story."

Story

Chapter 3 - The Story

Bob felt the dog licking his hand. His head hurt badly as he muttered, "Go away." The dog started to whine and licked Bob's face. Bob yelled, "Zack, let your dog out." No answer came. The dog jumped around desperate to be let outside. Suddenly Bob became awake enough to remember the night before and realized his son wasn't home. "Alright, you pain, I'm moving to let you out."

Bob opened the door and the dog ran outside fast. Due to his pounding headache, Bob laid down on the couch and closed his eyes. He thought about what happened the night before. His ex-wife and her new husband, that long ago was Bob's best friend, showed up and took his son away.

MIA TENROC

Bob had gotten his high school sweetheart Judy pregnant their senior year. He liked Judy well enough. She was the best of the girls that lived in the area, which didn't mean much. Bob considered most of the girls in their little town in Kentucky to be dumb and ugly. Judy was just fun for the time being. When she told him that she was with child, he tried to pretend it wasn't his. He knew the truth and so did everyone in town. His parents and hers forced the marriage.

He got a job in the mine but hated going there every day. He rented a small house for them to live in and provided the necessities but the rest of the money was his to go out and party with on the weekend.

Judy hoped they would have more kids and do the normal family activities but Bob wasn't ready to settle down. He gave enough of his life to her. He wanted to go to honky-tonks and play, sing and enjoy life. Judy gave up hope and filed for a divorce. Now all she did was want more money and hound him to spend more time with the boy.

Bob decided enough was enough. He quit his job, and when he got Zack for the weekend visit, he took off. The boy was only 2 at the time. Zack cried some for his mother but Bob told him that his mother had died. A 2-year-old forgets easily and within a week, there was no more mention of his mother.

FLAWED DECISIONS MURDER

Bob found work playing his music or working jobs for cash. Bob was hot-looking and women threw themselves at him. He would live with them, especially if they were rich. He was never faithful so most relationships ended quickly.

Zack had to write an autobiography for school. He asked questions about where he was born, if he had any relatives, and what they did for a living. Bob tried to be evasive about the subject, hoping Zack wouldn't look into it too much. Obviously, Zack did. Using the computer at school, he managed to track down his mother.

Bob started laughing at how mad she was when he opened the door. Zack came out with his bags already packed so this meeting had been well planned. Bob asked if Zack really wanted to leave with this stranger. Zack replied, "Knowing how much you lied to me, I think you aren't the man I know but the stranger instead."

That ungrateful brat just walked out the door. After all Bob did for him, to turn on him like that. Dudley, his one-time friend, grabbed him by the collar, "The only reason I'm not pounding the hell out of you is because of your son. What you put Judy through all these years was cruel. You took away the chance for her to see her child grow up and share her love. She made me promise to not harm you for the sake of Zack. I will respect that but not because you don't deserve to be taken down a notch."

After they left, Bob laughed and drank. He actually liked the boy but lately he'd been getting mouthy. Bob remembered how difficult he was as a teenager and was glad to not go through those years with his son. He expects his son to come running back after a few months of his mother's nagging. For now, for the first time in his life, Bob was free.

Story

Chapter 4 – Bob's New Life

Bob suddenly realized that the dog was gone. They had only gotten it a couple of weeks ago from the pound. He thought Shaggy would be good company for his son. The dog was good enough but the constant need for attention drove them both nuts. The other big problem was the dog always pulling a Houdini. He would disappear every time it went outside no matter how secure the yard was fenced in.

Bob grabbed the leash and after checking to determine that the yard was empty, he started walking down the street shouting the dog's name. While walking past a small church in the neighborhood, he heard Shaggy's bark as a reply to his call. Around the corner of the building came the most beautiful woman Bob ever saw. She was petite with long, wavy blonde

MIA TENROC

hair. The angel was dressed in a white gauze gown that floated which added to her spiritual flow. Shaggy was on a leash by her side. Bob knew women would be moved by his looks but never had it been in reverse. Bob had broad shoulders, a slim waist, black hair with crystal blue eyes. He knew how to turn on the charm and was going to do his best to win this one over.

"Hi. I'm Bob. My dog seems happier with you than he does with me."

"Lisette," she said as she extended a hand to shake. "I'm an assistant pastor here at the church." Bob noticed the small, plain gold band on her left hand. He hoped it was one like a Nun would wear, as if being married to God. She continued, "I've never seen you before. I take it you haven't attended our church."

Bob answered, "I'm newer to the neighborhood. I got the dog for my son since he didn't have any friends yet. The dog really hasn't taken to either of us yet. In fact, all he does is run away."

Lisette smiled, "I like children and hope to have one someday, but so far that hasn't worked out for me. How old is your son?"

Bob regretted mentioning him. "He's 13. He had recently developed some health issues. His mother and I are divorced. She lives near a good medical

FLAWED DECISIONS MURDER

treatment center so he left last night to live with her. I'm so heartbroken that I can't be with them but I need to stay and work to maintain his insurance and help pay the bills. There are times a parent has to do the right thing, not necessarily what he wants to do. I will be talking to him daily so he knows I love him but I don't think he's going to make it." Bob managed to force a tear and a sad look.

Lisette gave him a hug, "You poor dear man! You're being so brave and caring. I bet you are really hurting inside. Please let me know if there is anything that I can do for you. Why don't you come to church tomorrow? It's my Sunday to preach. Maybe you will feel uplifted."

Bob took advantage of the hug. He held her close. "Thank you for the hug. The contact of another caring soul has lifted my spirits." The result was what he hoped for as she continued to hold him close. Bob continued, "I really can't say that Jesus and I are on good terms right now."

Lisette released the hold. "Didn't you see the name on the church sign? At the 'House of Spirits', we worship those that have passed away before us. Maybe a past relative or loved one will hear your call and be there to guide your son."

Bob agreed to attend the service the next day. As he walked away, he thought that whole spirit worship thing sounded weird but if he could get another hug from Lisette, it would be worth it to attend.

Story

Chapter 5 – New Hope

Bob didn't own a suit so he dressed in black slacks and a blue shirt to help bring out his eyes. His hair was longer, about ear length, and perfectly styled. He never had his hopes so high for success with a woman than he did that morning, "Bobby boy, you are in love. Butterflies in the stomach and all." He decided to walk to the church since it was only a few blocks. There were about 20 cars in the parking lot so Bob checked his watch to make sure he was there at the right time.

Lisette was getting out of her car, waved, and called him over. "Bob, I'm so glad you came today. This is my husband, Richard. I need to get inside to prepare, so Richard will be glad to show you around."

MIA TENROC

Bob hoped he hid his disappointment as he extended his hand to say hello. "My pleasure, Richard. Thanks for helping me get acquainted."

Richard responded, "Call me Rich. That's what my friends do." He was watching his wife float into the church. "I think my life matches my name."

Bob wondered if Richard could read his mind on how much he wanted Lisette. Rich opened the door for Bob and explained, "To the left is the sanctuary. We start by having coffee and snacks before the service in the fellowship room to the right. We will then go into the sanctuary to meditate and invite the spirits to come, followed by songs and a sermon." There were about 30 adults and two teenagers in the room. "Let me introduce you around. Helena, she is our senior pastor and Grace is her daughter, this is Bob. His first visit here, ladies. This is Guy and Susan. Here is Violet. She is Native American so she's named after the first thing her mother saw after her birth. I heard you were divorced. Lottie is our resident husband seeker. She inherited a lot of money but never found love. Just a friendly warning but honestly she is a very nice person."

Bob was sick of the introductions and looking for Lisette. He tried not to be too obvious. They entered the sanctuary and he still didn't see her. "I thought your wife was preaching today but she's not here."

FLAWED DECISIONS MURDER

Rich didn't notice the interest. "She prepares with quiet time in meditation and prayer. Now we do the same. The people standing on the side might come and put their hands on you to help with any healing you might need."

Bob just gave a curious look out of the corner of his eye and looked straight ahead. Soon one of the ladies came over and had her hand hover about six inches behind the back of his head. He continued to stare forward but as she walked away, he turned his head and gave her a slight smile. He thought "I don't know what healing she thought I needed, but I don't feel any different."

Soon two more people, a man and a woman, went on the stage. The man pointed to a lady in the front row. "I see the spirit of a man about 50 years old, brown hair with gray starting to come in on the sides. He looks very distinguished. Does this sound like someone you might know? He sends a message. You have a big decision to make. He said the answer will come soon so you will know what to do. The decision will be made for you."

The lady spoke next. She pointed to a man. "I see the spirit of an elderly lady with her hair in a bun. She is wearing an apron over her dress as if she is about to cook. She said to tell you that money will come your way to pay for a car repair."

The man responded with sounds of joy. "That is welcome news!"

The man and woman took turns talking to other spirits and delivering their messages. The lady went last. She pointed at Bob. "I see a man that is older. He is dressed like he is doing car repair. He has on a cap and glasses. Does that sound like someone you know?"

Bob answered, "Yes." He chuckled to himself that the description would match anyone's dad or grandfather.

The woman continued, "He says you are looking for love. He said you will find it."

Lottie looked excited but didn't say anything. Bob just nodded. With Lisette, I already did, he thought to himself.

Lisette walked to the piano, sat down and began playing, singing with the voice of an angel. She announced, "Our next song is number 150 in the hymnals 'What a friend we have in Spirit'. Let us begin." Bob recognized the song being sung as a Christian hymn, only with the words 'God' and 'Jesus' changed to 'Spirit'.

After a couple of songs, she went on stage and gave a sermon about looking for the best and keeping a positive attitude. If it wasn't for his heart desire

FLAWED DECISIONS MURDER

delivering the message, he would have told these people they were a bunch of weirdos and walked out. Instead, he just smiled.

Lisette came over and gave him a hug. It wasn't as touching and personal as the day before because her husband was standing right there. "I hope that was an encouraging message for you."

Bob assured her it was.

Rich said, "Lisette and I are both here for you if there is anything we can do to help."

Phone numbers were exchanged, then Bob walked home thinking that there was still hope.

Abletown

Chapter 6 – Suspicious Women

About two days after Belinda started working on Leon's campaign, she came to see Jean in her room at the Friend's Home. "I know this is an unusual time to come visit but I wanted to talk to you privately about something. You know how your stories often follow real life. Leon is a really nice man. He was a big city mayor before retiring and moving here. The only reason he is running for office is to keep Abletown as the peaceful, quaint town it has always been. He actually likes Peter but doesn't agree with his idea of letting builders have whatever they want at the expense of the citizens. Remember on your story how Bob thinks he is desired by all the women he meets? There is a woman named Missy, about 35 and good looking, that volunteers at the campaign headquarters.

FLAWED DECISIONS MURDER

She flirts with Leon a lot. To my knowledge, Leon hasn't reacted to those flirtations but you can tell he enjoys them. He smiles at her differently than the rest of us. He sucks in his stomach and tries to puff out his chest. I hate to see a man ruin his career and lose the election just because he can't control his manly urges."

Jean listened carefully. "I've seen that with men many times in my life. Have you tried to talk to him about how her flirting appears to others? Have you mentioned his wife in front of the woman? Leon is a lucky man to have such a supporting wife that has been by his side for years."

Belinda nodded yes. "I ask him how his wife is doing every day. I scheduled his speaking engagement at the church next week and verified that his wife will be coming with him. Like I said, to my knowledge, he isn't taking the flirting seriously but I think it is an ego boosting thing for him. I just can't see why Missy is in the office. She doesn't talk to the other workers nor does she live in town. She claims that she has followed his career and thinks he is a good man. I'm thinking there is more to the story."

Jean suggested, "Why don't you write down her car model and license number and any other information you know. I will do what I can to check her out."

MIA TENROC

After Belinda left, Jean went for a walk to Eve's house on Third Street. Eve was equally surprised at the visit since the ladies had been together all day. Jean told Eve about the mystery woman at Leon's headquarters. "Do you want to help me do a little spying?"

Eve was all for it but then asked, "What can I do? If you want a car traced, wouldn't you be better off asking your husband-in-all-but-name, Nick? After all, he is a police detective."

Jean shook her head no. "I wouldn't want to involve him since there is no crime. He could get in trouble investigating someone that isn't a suspect in a case. I was hoping you would start working at Peter's campaign headquarters and try to get a look at his accounting books. I want to make sure he isn't paying Missy to work for Leon to get information on him. It could be Peter is paying her or knows who she is. I'm also concerned about his fund raising. Since this is such a small town, money isn't needed for our elections. Right now, you have stayed non-committed on either party. Priscilla knows I'm not in Peter's corner on this election and if I go in, she will suspect my motives."

Eve looked very serious. "The truth is I'm not sure who I support, though I am leaning toward Peter. I respect Belinda and her opinion, hence why I don't

FLAWED DECISIONS MURDER

speak out against her ideas. I actually would like to know the truth for sure. I'm skeptical to the idea that Peter would work dishonestly against Leon, but I will report the truth no matter what I find."

Jean saw Gwen pull up and get out of her car. She asked Eve, "Has your neighbor talked to you yet? Is she any friendlier?"

Eve laughed, "Not at all. She still hasn't said a word to anyone but Fannie. Fannie is playing that for all its worth. A few people from the diner stopped in Fannie's shop to ask questions but they got no answers. Fannie tells them to not judge people so quickly."

Jean replied, "I do agree with that statement but it is still odd, since you are such a kind person, for Gwen not to even wave or be pleasant."

Abletown

Chapter 7 – Gwen Speaks

Eve was stressed and feeling a little guilty. She walked home after working at Peter's office. As she approached her house, she noticed her car was gone. Shocked and afraid her car was stolen, she stood on the curb with her hands on her hips, trying to get her thoughts in order of what to do. Eve was about to check with Jo, who lived next door, to see if she knew anything about the car, when Gwen came out of the house and walked over to her.

Gwen extended her hand in introduction. "Hi, I'm Gwen. I apologize for not being friendlier before. I'm in a bad space right now and am avoiding interaction with people. I saw a woman about 30 with brown hair, about 5 foot 5 and on the heavy side but not really fat.

FLAWED DECISIONS MURDER

She drove off with your car. Does that describe anyone you know?"

Eve pulled out her phone to show a picture of her daughter to Gwen when she noticed a text, that she hadn't heard come in. It was from her daughter saying that her car wouldn't start and that she had a doctor's appointment at a special clinic that was about 50 miles away. Her daughter's friend wasn't willing to drive her that far, but agreed to bring her over to pick up Eve's car. Eve pulled up a picture of her daughter and showed it to Gwen.

"That was the girl," Gwen said. "Who is she?"

Eve said without enthusiasm, "My daughter. She sent a text." Eve's phone rang, "It's my daughter. Please excuse me while I take this."

Gwen remained and watched as Eve's face turned red with anger. "Are you all right?"

Eve was shouting at the phone, "I can't believe you did this to me again." Eve hung up with tears in her eyes, "I'm so sorry to get to meet you and have all this happen. My daughter isn't supposed to drive my car, that is why she took it without asking."

Gwen suggested, "Why don't we go to my house and get you some tea."

Eve said nothing more until she had a cup of tea in front of her. Then she explained, "My granddaughter lived with me a few months and had a key to my house. She gave it to her mother, who used it to get my spare car keys. My daughter has wrecked my cars before. She runs red lights, stop signs, and toll booths. My insurance is through the roof because of her. I don't turn my back on her. I would have driven her to the appointment but I would never let her drive my car there. Now she has wrecked it again. I better call the insurance company. Thank you so much for your kindness, being there to support me just now."

Gwen answered, "You're welcome. I have my own problems with my family so I understand what you are going through."

Eve called the insurance company and explained the situation. She was given the alternative of either pressing charges against her daughter for taking the car without permission or getting her insurance canceled. Eve called her husband, Nigel, and told him the story.

Nigel had his usual negative response, "I would press charges. You need insurance and she should suffer the consequences of her actions. You were always too permissive of a parent. Make her suffer from the result of her action, not you."

Eve hung up. There was no way she could put her daughter in jail for grand theft auto. She called the

FLAWED DECISIONS MURDER

insurance company back. Eve was informed that the car was totaled. She would receive a check for the value of the car. Eve said, "Thank you for the check and please cancel the policy."

Later that day, Eve arrived at Jean's home on her new Moped. Jean and her significant other, Nick, was sitting on the porch and came down to see Eve's new ride. Eve admitted, "I hoped to talk to you about my newest problem but it can wait until tomorrow."

Nick invited Eve to stay, "I would be glad to listen."

Eve spilled out her story, "I just can't put my daughter in jail. I know she did something very wrong but I can't destroy her life over it."

Nick was the one to reply, "You're right that it would be hard to overcome a criminal charge. Do you really think you can get by in life on a small engine like this one? What about bringing in groceries? What happens if you have to go out in stormy weather?"

Eve started to cry, "I don't know. I will take it one day at a time. In a small town like this one, I walk most places. I guess I will just shop for a couple of days at a time so I can carry the groceries in a backpack. I think the most upsetting thing is Nigel wanting me to press charges. He blames me for what has happened. I could use a little support, not criticism."

MIA TENROC

Nick gave Eve a hug. "That is an understandable feeling. It looks like you thought of the shopping part. You can just work from home when the weather is nasty. The good thing about the Moped is you could pay cash so no monthly bill. Also, with the small motor size, you don't have to carry insurance. That will save you a ton of money. Also, another good point is you can lock the Moped in your shed and keep the key with you. Just let Jean and I know if you need to go somewhere far from town and we will be glad to help drive you."

Jean didn't say anything because Nick pretty much had it covered. Jean did warn, "I use to drive a motorcycle and it is very dangerous. People don't see you for some reason and often pull out in front of you."

Eve smiled, "That's why I bought a hot pink one. I figured it would get noticed. Maybe I'll put balloons or something on it when I drive to create more attention." They all laughed.

Jean asked, "Did you get to know Gwen? Was she nice?"

Eve was happy to reply, "Yes, she was very nice. We didn't get to talk much but she invited me over. I think I will show her my new ride. My daughter and granddaughter can't even ride a bicycle so at least no one will want to take my new vehicle."

31

FLAWED DECISIONS MURDER

Nick said to Jean as Eve pulled away, "I didn't know you rode motorcycles."

Jean looked at him seriously, "I did when I was in my late teens. I have no desire to ride one now."

Nick smiled, "I do. I use to ride when I was young but thinking about it is giving me the urge again. The police have a motorcycle club. I think I will see about going for a ride with them one day."

Story

Chapter 8 – Bob's Problems

Bob went out and tried to start his car so he could head to the store. There was no reaction to the turn of the key. Cursing his luck, he got out and popped the hood. No matter what he adjusted or tried to do, he couldn't get the car to work. Lottie was driving by. "I'm on my way to the church for meditation classes. Would you like to join us?"

Bob could hardly hide his anger but wanted to make a good impression. "No, thank you for asking, but I need to get my car problems solved."

Lottie pulled over and got out of her car. "Nothing more frustrating than car problems. I have AAA if you would like me to call for help. Were you heading somewhere in a hurry? They seem to take a while to get here sometimes."

FLAWED DECISIONS MURDER

Bob agreed to the help. Lottie made the call. Bob said, "Thank you for your kindness. I was just going to get groceries. I guess I could get by without for now. Did you want to go on to the class?"

Lottie informed him. "I have to be here. It has to be my car or a car I'm riding in." The response to the call was only about 20 minutes. Lottie tried to keep Bob engaged in conversation the entire time.

The mechanic said, "This isn't anything I can fix here. Do you want the car towed?"

Lottie was the one to reply, "Yes, please. Here is the name and address of the body shop I use." Lottie turned to Bob, "They are very honest and reasonable in price." Bob consented to the suggestion.

After the tow truck left, Bob said, "You can still make the end of the class."

Lottie tucked her arm through Bob's. "And leave you stranded? No way! Why don't we go to the store now?"

Bob was on the point of being obligated so he agreed. At the store, he said, "I don't cook much. I'm good at steaks. Would you like me to make steaks and baked potatoes as a thank you?"

Lottie was thrilled and accepted the invitation. It was a pleasant evening but Bob was careful to keep his distance and make it like friends being there for each other. He didn't want to give the impression of being interested in Lottie. Bob also didn't want to ruin his chances with Lisette if there were any. He didn't want a reputation of being a womanizer at the church.

Lottie asked, "Do you need a ride to work tomorrow?"

Bob explained, "I work close by so I can walk to work in the morning. I'm sure someone will give me a ride home." Bob actually did day labor. He never worked a regular job because his ex-wife would be able to find him by his social security number. He mowed lawns, worked jobs that paid cash and lived off rich women for the most part. He didn't want Lottie dropping him off at the day labor office.

Bob got up a little late the next morning and by the time he walked to work, he was too late to get a job. He also got a call from the auto repair. The list of things needed for the car was thousands of dollars. He had to explain he couldn't afford the repairs at this time and that he would contact them tomorrow. Bob was feeling very low.

Lottie dropped by that night. "I talked to the auto repair and they said you told them to wait on the work. I know you need a car so I told them to go ahead and do the work and I would pay for it. I don't know if you know this but I'm very comfortable when it comes to finances."

FLAWED DECISIONS MURDER

Bob used the lie about his son as an excuse, "Helping to pay for my son's medical bill is my first priority. I know you mean well but I'm embarrassed to have you help me. I will pay you back."

Since he no longer has a reason to hide, the next morning Bob went to many businesses and applied for a job, but after years with no employment, he was turned down immediately at each place. He missed another day of work as a day labor. This went on for a week.

Lottie stopped by each day, usually with a dinner she had prepared. The landlord stopped by and told Bob, "You own two months back rent. Here is an eviction notice."

Lottie started to get up and intervene but Bob waived her back. After the landlord left, Bob said, "I don't need this big house since it's just me. I will get a room somewhere for a lot less money a month. I will be honest, I'm out of work right now and not having much luck finding a job. Good employment is what I really need, not a handout."

Lottie suggested, "The church is looking for a custodian but it is only part-time. I bet they would be glad to give you the job. It doesn't pay enough to live. Are you handy around the house? I need some repairs done on my home. You can stay there. I have four bedrooms so it's not like I'm saying we will live

MIA TENROC

together but you can be at the house and do the repairs while I'm at work."

Bob, feeling like he was out of options, said, "I would like that very much." Inside, he had a gut feeling that it would be a big mistake. He always lived by the opportunities that came his way and no other offers was available to him.

Lottie made the call to the two leaders of the church, Helena and Lisette. They called an emergency meeting and the decision to hire Bob was completed that night.

Story

Chapter 9 – Fallout

Bob's first day on the job as janitor for the church was received with some controversy unbeknown to him. Richard was very upset because he could see how much Bob wanted his wife. Had Richard known about the vote, he would have raised an objection to the appointment. He didn't want to say anything directly to his wife because he didn't want to appear jealous. He loved his wife and he really did trust her. It was Bob he didn't trust. He stopped by the office to speak to Bob. "Hi, I understand you got a job here. I hope this helps your situation."

Bob replied, "I hate to admit how bad my situation has become. I've not been able to find a job. I need to send money to help my son, and thus got behind on my rent. I've been kicked out of the house."

MIA TENROC

"Really," said Richard with much interest. He recalled Bob telling Lisette he had to stay here to work a job with insurance for his son. He continued, "Where are you going to live?"

Bob turned a little red, "I've moved in with Lottie for the time being. We aren't living together but she wants a bathroom remodeled and I know how to do it. With my car being repaired, it seemed like the best solution was to live where I'm going to do work. Lottie paid for the car repairs so I owe her a lot of money for that. The remodeling should help with that debt. I'm an honest man and like to pay what I owe to people."

Richard was a little torn if he should believe Bob or not. Yes, Bob is in lust for Lisette but so far, Richard had no proof that he was dishonorable. "It's nice that you are able to help each other. Lottie has no money problems but does need someone to help her with the house. I hope things work out for you."

Richard left with a plan. As soon as he got in the car, Richard called Lottie. "I just talked to Bob. He seems excited and thankful about the opportunities you have given him."

Lottie answered, "That's good to hear. I'm at work so I can't talk much now. Keep me posted secretly of course if he says anything further." She hung up with a smile on her lips. Bob was a good-

FLAWED DECISIONS MURDER

looking man and would be a good catch for her. She was rich and deserved arm candy to take to events.

Violet had come to the church to drop off flowers for the alter. She overhead the conservation but remained hidden. After Richard departed, she entered the office Bob was working on. "Hi. I don't know if you remember, I'm Violet."

Bob looked up and gave a genuine smile. "Yes, I remember. You're the Native American. I wondered why you came to this church instead of one on the reservation."

Violet had a look like she could see straight through you. She replied shyly, "I'm a transplant. I'm from a tribe in the Oklahoma area. I don't feel welcome on the reservation. I moved here because of my job. This church doesn't really have any rules of belief. You can worship who or what you want. This makes it so I can practice my faith. Why are you here? I don't sense any faith in you. Sorry, I didn't mean to be rude."

Bob laughed, "You are very bright. I'm feeling very alone right now. I also don't fit into a regular church. I'm here more for the companionship than the religious belief."

"You have much to look out for. I heard you say you moved in with Lottie. She is after a man. Everyone here has their oddities but, in the end, we

MIA TENROC

are there for each other." Violet didn't say that she observed Bob lustful looks at Lisette. She hoped he understood her warning.

Bob liked Violet and her honesty. "You say this church didn't really have rules. What do you mean?"

Violet sat and looked at him. "The Preachers do a correspondence course. It contains principles of life. They really follow the ten commandments. Even our music is a ripoff of the Christian music. People come here because there is some reason they wouldn't be accepted in a Christian church. Mine is following the faith of my ancestors. Some of the people here are gays or lesbians that don't feel accepted at other churches. Some are here because they lost someone and are hoping that speaking to spirits are real. Some hope to be selected by spirits to be mediums."

Bob leaned in and whispered, "I take it you don't believe in any of this."

Violet smiled, "I know spirits are real. I just don't believe most people here have the gift." She got up and left without even saying good-bye.

Abletown

Chapter 10 – Eve's Curiosity

After hearing this part of Jean's story, it triggered Eve's curiosity again. She stopped at the diner and picked up a pie. She stood on Gwen's porch trying to get the nerve to knock. Gwen was nice last time but that wasn't her normal behavior.

Gwen opened the door with caution but smiled upon seeing Eve. "Come in."

Eve extended the pie, "I wanted to say thank you for being supportive of me the other day. I guess you can tell that I have family problems. I suppose you don't want to hear about that so I won't burden you. I just wanted to let you know I appreciate the friendship you displayed."

MIA TENROC

Gwen said, "I don't mind if you want to vent. That was a very rude thing for your daughter to do."

Eve felt free to spill everything. "My daughters are from a previous marriage. I always felt bad that their father wanted nothing to do with them. I spoiled them because I was trying to make up for the love he didn't provide. My husband, Nigel, and I have been married for 15 years and the girls and my husband don't like each other. I'm often stuck in the middle."

Gwen looked surprised, "Not that I was spying but I never noticed a man at your house. I thought you lived alone."

Eve laughed, "I do. That's the only way I can stay married. My husband is a hoarder. We had to move from our last home in the city because of the constant notices from the zoning board about all his junk. I bought a farm about 10 miles from here where there are no regulations. He lives there with his things. I love a neat and clean house so my little house here works perfectly. We visit when we want to be together. It's more like dating and it keeps us from arguing so much. What about you? I haven't seen anyone here so do you also live alone?"

Gwen confessed, "My husband and I just went through a divorce. Just the normal story of a man falling in love with the secretary. Of course, the new wife, which he married the day after our divorce, is

FLAWED DECISIONS MURDER

half my age. I don't believe she loves him at all. He is a doctor and makes very good money. I'm a nurse who works long hours a few days a week. My children say they think I drove my husband away because I'm too cold and factual. That has caused a friction between us. I decided to sweep all of them out of my life. That's why my license plate says 'broom'. I swept away the negative people I feel are attacking me. I moved to a small town instead of a big city. I got a new house and only brought a few possessions with me. I want everything new."

Eve stood up and gave Gwen a hug. "Well, I'm glad to say I'm a new friend so you don't have to sweep me out."

Gwen laughed. "I've been hearing all the rumors about me being a witch around town. I assure you, I'm a Methodist but for now unchurched. I don't want to go back to where my family and I attended together."

Eve said, "I want you to meet my friends. Belinda and Jean are active with the Methodist church here in town. They would be glad to take you there and introduce you around. We do water aerobics at the Friend's Home. If you like, you can come with me. It's great exercise and good company. I don't mean to be pushy but if you would like to go, you are always welcome."

MIA TENROC

Gwen said, "I gotten to know Fannie at the second-hand store. She told me the same thing. I think I will join you but maybe in a few weeks. I'm still in recovery right now."

Eve said, "Is what you told me a secret? I mean about the license plate."

Gwen laughed saying, "Fannie told me not to tell anyone to keep the town occupied with something to gossip about. If you want to tell, I guess it's not really a secret. Just don't make me sound bad if you tell it, please."

Abletown

Chapter 11 – Secrets

Eve jumped on her scooter and drove to the Friend's Home to hear the next installment of the story Jean was telling. The other ladies laughed when they saw Eve sporting a black leather jacket and a helmet that had pink and black butterflies on it.

Jean said, "Good job. I bet people will notice you when you come down the street. We were waiting for you before continuing with the story. You know the answer, don't you?"

Eve looked innocent, "What do you mean, the answer?"

Jean quizzed her, "Nothing happens in this town without everyone noticing it. You went into the diner and bought a pie. When you got to Third Street, you

MIA TENROC

went to Gwen's home, not your own. I can tell by the look on your face that you know the secret of the license plate."

Eve acted defiant, "You can't know that I know." Jean continued to stare at her. "Ok, ok, I confess. I do know but I can't believe I'm showing that fact." Jean continued to stare. "Gwen is really nice. She just went through a divorce and is starting her life over. She didn't even want her possessions because she wants to sweep her life clean. I'm beginning to think that's a good idea. Between the stupid things my daughter does and the lack of support from my husband, I think I should make a clean sweep as well. Did you know that Fannie knew the truth and didn't tell anyone?"

Jean smiled, "That doesn't surprise me. I can see Fannie wanting to drag this joke out on the town as long as possible. I can't say I knew for sure about Fannie because she has a poker face. You, on the other hand, had a smug smile like you knew a secret. Changing the subject, what are you doing Saturday?"

Eve answered, "No plans. Why?"

Jean said, "Because your little scooter has Nick hearing the call of the wild. He borrowed a motorcycle from a friend that will be on vacation. He arranged for us to ride with the Blue Knights, the police motorcycle club. I figured, since this was your doing, that you could ride with us."

FLAWED DECISIONS MURDER

"I get to ride my Pinkie with the big boys?"

Jean shook her head no. "Pinkie, as you are apparently calling your scooter, can't keep up with the big boys but one of the other guys will let you ride behind him. We will take a picnic lunch and go to Lookout Mountain Park."

Eve was happy, "That sounds like fun."

Jean continued, "Since we know the broom isn't about being a witch, I guess that means my story is wasted."

Belinda jumped into the conversation, "I'm enjoying the story. We don't need a reason for it. By the way, where is Priscilla? Isn't she going to be here for story time?"

Jo said, "Since I haven't revealed how I'm going to vote, Priscilla felt safe to call me to make her excuses for not coming. She said she has a meeting with the attorney for the trust fund today. Even though we are all on the board for the trust, she said it was personal and there was no need for us to be there. I thought it was odd that she called me when Jean lives next door to her. I guess Priscilla didn't want to tell Jean to her face, fearing she would get the stare down just like Eve did."

The ladies continued through their normal day of tea at Fannie's store and then water aerobics. After the group went their separate ways for the day, Jean drove to Leon's headquarters and waited outside in her car. Belinda was already inside. She called Jean and told her, "That person leaving is Missy." Jean watched Missy go to her car and then followed her up the highway to town. Her plan was to trail a little further each day. Jean would see what exit Missy took off the highway and then wait there the next day to trail her further. Missy was so busy talking on the phone and playing with the radio that Jean felt sure that Missy didn't know she was being tailed. The exit Missy took was in a very seedy part of town. She pulled into one of those monthly rental hotels and Jean continued on down the street.

Jean planned to come back the next day with Belinda to continue the investigation after story time.

Story

Chapter 12 – Music

Bob liked going to the church to work in order to avoid Lottie. She was really nice but he felt she was smothering him. He actually liked a lot of the people at the church and enjoyed talking to them. Bob was talking to Lonny, one of the musicians at the church, when a call came in for him. "Lonny, is everything alright?" asked Bob.

Lonny answered, "I have a country band. We do little gigs at clubs around town. It's more for spending money and fun. We don't plan to try to make it big. I just got news that our lead guitarist hurt his hand in an accident at work. We are supposed to play in a few hours."

Bob patted him on the back, "You're in luck. I can play any type of guitar and sing good too. I've

MIA TENROC

played at clubs all my life. I'm available if you would like me to join you."

Lonny said, "That sounds great. Let me call the other guys and make sure no one else arranged anything." He came back into the room a few minutes later, "I really appreciate your offer. The band would love to have you sit in tonight. Hopefully we can pull this off with never having practiced together."

Bob called Lottie, "I won't be home for dinner tonight. I have to finish up here, stop by the house to get my guitar, and play with a band tonight. I really feel bad being in debt to you and picking up gigs will help me pay you back sooner."

Lottie greeted him at the door with a sandwich packed. She asked, "Where are you playing tonight?"

Bob didn't want her to show up so he said, "A private club from what I'm told."

Lottie suggested, "I would love to hear you play. Maybe I could come in with the band."

Bob tried to ignore her but she persisted, "This is my first job with the band. Not only will it be difficult to pick up on the music and their style, I don't want to be asking favors." Lottie looked hurt but accepted the decision.

The night went perfect. The band sounded like they had been together for years. Bob asked to do a

FLAWED DECISIONS MURDER

solo song and it was a major hit. Many of the ladies at the club made passes at him. That was a great boost to Bob's ego. The band asked him to play until their regular guitarist returned. It was going to be at least six weeks. Bob acted calmly while he agreed to do so. The truth was Bob was in heaven.

Lottie pretended not to be waiting up for him, but as he walked down the hall, she came out of her room. "I'm sorry. I heard the door and got up to make sure it was you." Lottie had left her robe hanging open to show a see-through gown.

Bob pretended not to notice, "I'm so sorry I scared you. It's very late and you have to be at work early tomorrow. I will be really quiet and get into my bed immediately. Good night."

Lottie asked, "Do you think it will be too much on you with working at the church, working here on my bathroom, and playing at clubs at night?"

Bob assured her it wouldn't be. "My main work at church is on Sunday night. I am also doing a few hours after meditation on Monday and after service on Wednesday, which are both evening hours. The clubs will be Thursday, Friday and Saturday from 8:00 p.m. until 2:00 a.m. I have all day during the week to work on your house. Besides, one bathroom is only about two weeks work at the most. Thanks again for all that you are doing for me and good night."

MIA TENROC

Lottie took the dismissal fine in front of him. Behind the closed door she said to herself, "I've got to find out where he is performing. I don't want to lose this one."

Story

Chapter 13 – Lottie's Hunt

Lottie showed up at the church looking very happy. She wanted everyone to think her joy was from getting a new boyfriend. She saw Lisette and asked, "Did you know Bob is a musician? He had a gig last night and it went very well."

Lisette looked surprised, "No, I didn't know that. Maybe he will have something to contribute to our service here at the church. I will have to ask him about that."

Lottie went up to a couple of other people that performed music for the church but no one knew about Bob performing.

Bob arrived at the church ready for the service. He was trying his best not to show his desire for

MIA TENROC

Lisette. He shook hands with Richard and Lisette. As he moved through the fellowship hall, Lonny took him aside. "Lottie is trying to find out about the gig last night. She doesn't know you are playing in my band, I guess. She went up to three other people trying to find out where you played. I didn't say anything. You do realize that she is man-crazy in a scary way?"

Bob nodded yes. "Thanks man. I got in a bad spot and she is helping me out. I'm making sure there is nothing going on between us but she isn't getting the hint that I'm not interested. I try not to let her know what I'm doing because I don't want her to feel she has ownership over me."

Lonny said, "Good plan but if I was you, I would move out as soon as you get that bathroom done."

When they went in for the spirit readings, the person on the stage said, "I'm getting a message but I don't know who it's for. It's an older man that looks like he spent a lot of years on the road. He states that love is about to bloom in this church. Take it to heart if this applies to you and good luck." Lottie touched her neck. She was so sure that this message was for her and Bob. She looked at him to give him a smile but he was looking at Lisette as she sat down at the piano for her songs.

Lottie's overreaction wasn't lost on Violet. After the service, she delivered the same warning to Bob

FLAWED DECISIONS MURDER

that Lonny had. "Be careful. Lottie has an imagination instead of seeing reality. I can tell you're not interested in her but she thinks this is the beginning of a relationship."

Bob thanked Violet. "I really appreciate your concern. I actually have that same worry myself. If you can ever drop a hint to her, I would appreciate it."

Violet laughed, "I don't want to be involved."

Bob said sincerely, "It's funny that I feel so comfortable talking around you. I would never think of deceiving you. Do you have that calming effect on everyone?"

Violet nodded yes and walk away.

Richard, on the other hand, saw this as an opportunity. "Lottie, I'm sure that message was for you. I don't know if Bob sees it yet but you two are so good together. I wouldn't be too pushy but I would be persevering until he sees the truth." The truth was Richard didn't like Lottie but he saw it as a way to drive Bob away from the church and his wife.

After the worshipers left the building, Bob began his cleanup. He started in the worship side of the church and worked his way back to the fellowship hall. Violet was still there talking to a woman he didn't know. They looked up and said, "I guess we better get out of your way."

MIA TENROC

Bob finished mopping the kitchen floor. He looked up and saw the ladies still talking outside. He carried out the garbage as his final act of the day. He put his hands on his back and kind of stretched, not knowing he was being watched.

Violet came over and asked, "Your back hurting?"

Bob said, "Nothing that a warm shower won't fix."

Violet reached into her purse and pulled out a tin and handed it to him. "After your shower, rub a little of this on your back."

Bob looked at the tin. Violet answered his question before he could ask. "It's a natural ointment for aches and pains. My father is a medicine man. I run the marketing for his products in this part of the country as well as a private store for him. What he makes really works. He knows more about herb and plants than anyone I ever knew." She turned and left.

Abletown

Chapter 14 – Bike Day

Nick and Jean were looking forward to the ride since it was such a lovely day. Eve road with them to a private home. A man came out and opened the garage. There were two beautiful Harleys waiting for their use. Jean made the introductions. "Eve, this is Connor. He is part of the motorcycle force. You will ride on the back of his bike."

Eve pulled out her butterfly helmet to wear. Connor started laughing. "We sure will look tough going down the road with that on."

Eve defended herself, "I use it with my pink scooter so people will notice me."

The men tied the picnic baskets onto the bike rack and they mounted up and got on the open road.

MIA TENROC

Eve enjoyed her little Moped but she was really excited to feel the horsepower of the Harley purring down the street. She clung tight to Connor. He smelled amazing. He was tall with wide shoulder and a firm but slim waistline. Jean was clinging to Nick the same way but not because of feeling dreamy. Jean, having owned a motorcycle of her own, remembered the dangers of riding a bike.

They arrived at the park to find about a dozen other couples setting up their picnic lunches. Someone had driven a car in order to bring coolers loaded with beer and soft drinks. Someone else turned on music. Another person started a fire in the grill so after eating they could make smores. Everyone was laughing and having a lot of fun.

Nick suggested, "Why don't we walk up the trail to the lookout tower. I could use a little exercise after that big meal." Jean was all for it. Connor and Eve joined them.

Arriving at the tower, Eve elected not to climb the four flights of stairs to the top. The other three hurried up the steps. The two men were twice as fast but Jean wouldn't give up. She just moved a little slower.

Nick passed her on the way down, "There are two viewing glasses up there. Do you want me to go up with you?"

FLAWED DECISIONS MURDER

Jean said, "I will get up there soon. You don't have to do the climb again."

The two men were talking with Eve below while Jean looked through the glasses. She moved them around looking at all the scenery. Looking to the right, she noticed a cabin in the woods. She saw movement. She zoomed in to get a closer look. She was sure she saw Leon and a woman in the backyard. The woman's back was to Jean but she could tell that she took off a robe and had nothing on underneath. Leon turned to walk away. The woman grabbed him and tried to kiss him. Leon pushed her to the side. The woman stumbled and fell to the ground. Jean had a side view and was sure it was Missy. Leon made it to his car and left.

Missy grabbed the robe to put it on and was walking towards her car. Jean saw a flash in the bushes behind Missy. She saw the back of a man with what looked like a camera strap over his shoulder. Right then, the time limit ran out on the viewer. Jean got another quarter but when the viewer started working, she didn't see the man nor Missy. The car that Missy drove was just going around the corner and out of sight.

Nick yelled up, "Why are you taking so long? We are ready to head back to the party."

MIA TENROC

Jean replied, "Coming! I didn't realize I was taking so long."

When she reached the bottom, Nick immediately asked, "What's wrong? You look very upset."

Jean admitted, "I saw a naked woman." The others laughed.

Nick asked, "Did the woman want to be naked or was she forced to be?"

Jean didn't like to keep secrets from Nick but didn't want to say all that she thought she saw. "She wanted to be. She took her robe off and had nothing on underneath."

Nick continued the quizzing, "Was she alone?" Jean shook her head no. "What did the man do?"

Jean said in a low voice, "Turned and walked away."

Again, there was much laughter by the other three. Eve asked, "Was she fat or ugly?" Jean shook her head no again.

Connor said, "What is wrong with the guy, then?" There was no reply.

They joined the others and enjoyed the rest of the day. Jean could not get the scene out of her mind. She would check it out tomorrow with Belinda. She didn't

FLAWED DECISIONS MURDER

want to accuse Leon of doing something immoral with the upcoming election.

When they got back to Connor's house, Connor stood close to Eve and said, "Thank you for coming today. As you saw, everyone was in couples. I just got divorced and I'm not really dating anyone but I didn't want to go alone. Your company was a pleasure. I was worried with Jean doing the matchmaking. She has been known for her jokes."

Eve loved the feeling of standing close to Connor. "She didn't tell me it was a date. I'm married but I had a wonderful time. If you want a friend to go with you another time, I would be glad to accompany you."

Connor admitted, "Jean said you was married and this was just friends going out. I hope your husband didn't mind."

Eve looked sad, "I'm sure he wouldn't. We live separately but we are remaining faithful to each other. I can't tell you how much I enjoyed today. Thank you."

Abletown

Chapter 15 – Truth

The rest of the weekend was wonderful, but Nick could tell there was something wrong.

Jean tried to pass it off, "I don't like seeing naked people in the woods."

He chuckled, "I doubt they liked you spying on them. There's really nothing you can do about it. You can be a little prudish, you know. I wouldn't mind if you made love to me in the woods. Speaking of love in the woods, I know we each told Connor that Eve was married and just going out as a friend but they are quite taken with each other."

Jean smiled, "Of course, he is a hunk." Nick threw a pillow at her. They fell back into the bed laughing.

FLAWED DECISIONS MURDER

As soon as Nick left for work on Monday morning, Jean called Belinda. It was obvious that the call got her out of bed. Jean's voice displayed her panic, "I need to talk to you. I don't want anyone else to hear. Can I come over before we would normally meet on the porch?"

Belinda hated to get up early but she could tell by the tone of Jean's voice that it was urgent. "Sure. Come on over. I will prepare some coffee for me and tea for you."

Before Belinda could get downstairs, Jean was already there. Jean reported what she saw two days before. Belinda was surprised. "I can't say I'm shocked because men have this way of thinking young girls love them for who they are and not what they can provided for them. What did you find when you followed Missy the other day?"

Jean said, "She lives in a really bad part of town. Specifically, she lives in the red-light district. I haven't had time to go down to ask questions yet. I would prefer someone went with me because it's not a nice neighborhood. Fannie doesn't have the store open today so I was going to ask her. She would embrace the chance to interview ladies of the evening."

Belinda asked, "What should I do? Should I tell Leon what you saw?"

MIA TENROC

Jean tried to think, "The only benefit of telling him would be so he can protect himself from Missy and maybe prevent his wife from finding out about the incident. Maybe he can tell Missy not to come back."

Belinda suggested, "Maybe she won't come back after he turned her down. You would think she would feel like a fool. I will call you and let you know if she shows up. Let's make sure Priscilla doesn't know about this. I don't want to give her any ammunition. She has been acting so odd lately."

Jean sighed, "She has been avoiding everyone except Eve. If she finds out that Eve is spying for me then that friendship will end too."

Belinda was shocked at that news. "What do you mean spying?"

Jean confessed, "Eve really doesn't know who she is going to vote for. She wouldn't work for Peter's campaign since she isn't sure. I asked her to volunteer so she could get a look at the accounting figures if possible. After all, she did work with Peter on other matters to do with bookkeeping. If he isn't hiding something, he would have asked her to help. If he doesn't ask her, then that would mean he is keeping a secret. Don't tell anyone I told, including Eve. She agreed because she wants to do what is right but I think she feels a little guilty."

FLAWED DECISIONS MURDER

After a second cup of drink and more relaxing conversation, Belinda said, "I guess it is almost time for our story on the porch." While walking over, she continued, "It's funny how the story started off because of the broom license plate but now the similarities are about men's egos and women that are controlling and obsessive."

Priscilla came out of her apartment early. She knocked on Jean's door and got no answer, so she went to the porch. When she saw Belinda and Jean laughing together, she felt a sense of betrayal.

Story

Chapter 16 – Escape

Bob tried to act like everything was alright but in reality, he felt trapped. "I've got to think of a way to earn money and get out of here." At night, he would sleep with his door locked. Every night, he heard Lottie trying the handle to see if she could slip in and surprise him. Monday through Wednesday, he worked on finishing the bathroom project. He would stay in bed until he heard Lottie leave for work. He worked as fast as he could to make the job go by quickly.

Lonny reported to Lisette that not only was Bob a great guitar player but he was equally good at singing. "Lisette, if you put him on stage at the church, I think it will bring in people to see him." Lisette called to ask Bob if he would perform on Wednesday night when she led the service. He was thrilled to accept.

FLAWED DECISIONS MURDER

After a few weeks of watching the members of the church, he believed less than ever about their ability to contact spirits. He considered the members needy, searching for love and acceptance when in reality, they were being conned by Helena. He kept track of the money being donated and found it to be rather profitable. However, he did consider Lisette sincere and the real deal. They agreed to meet at the church early on Wednesday to practice a few songs. The 4:00 time was good since Richard would be working and they could be alone.

"Lisette," he said sincerely, "I'm really into this whole church thing. I'm thinking about becoming a Pastor. I went to the main church website and ordered the training material but they said I needed an active Pastor to be my sponsor. Would you be willing to do so?"

Lisette was very happy to hear the news, "I just knew when we met there was something special about you. I would love to but sadly I can't. Only the senior Pastor of the church can do that. I would be willing to talk to Helena about sponsoring you or if you prefer, we could approach her together."

Bob used the opportunity to give Lisette a hug. He was careful not to include passion. "I just don't know what I would have done without you the past few weeks. You brighten every life you enter. I think we should go over the songs one more time, if you don't mind. We make beautiful music together. I just want to make sure it's perfect so it paves the way for your message tonight."

Lisette hugged Bob back, "You are so considerate. I agree, one more time."

The service went smoothly and Bob's singing was a big hit. As usual, after the collection basket was passed, Bob slipped out of the service and hid in the cleaning closet that was off the fellowship hall and adjacent to the office. This was where the people who were going to talk to the spirits hid to overhear the members. There was a peep hole so they could see who was speaking and who to make their predictions to. When working in the church alone, Bob had put in a peep hole on the other side of the wall that looked into the church office. Grace would take the money into the office, count it, and make the deposit at the bank on the way home. She would honestly put down what the members contributed but any cash without a name on it made its way into her purse. After watching this for a few weeks, he had an estimate about how much was being taken.

After the service was over, Helena called him into the office. "Lisette tells me you want sponsorship to become a Pastor." Bob admitted he did. "I just

FLAWED DECISIONS MURDER

don't get the feeling you are sincere. Do you really think you can talk to spirits?"

Bob answered, "I know I can. I've had the gift all along but didn't understand it until I got informed about how it works in this church."

Helena challenged him, "Give me an example of a spirit speaking to you. What is one saying?"

Bob pretended to think. "I see the spirit of a woman that looks a lot like you but was a little shorter and about 55 when she passed. She has blue eyes, and salt and pepper hair. She said she worked with you in this church when it started." Lottie had told Bob all about Helena and her sister, Darlene. Darlene died about 5 years ago. Bob continued his act, "I keep getting a name like "Doris, Donna, no wait it is Darlene. I think she wants me to continue on the path to be a Pastor. She said she will make an exact provable prediction to prove it. She said that Grace has $45.00 in the zipper on the inside of her purse." Bob acted like the strain of the communication exhausted him.

Helena called out the door for her daughter to enter. "Grace, please let me see your purse." Grace looked suspiciously at Bob. Helena unzipped the purse. "Oh, my goodness, there is $45.00 in the side pocket. Bob told me that Darlene wants him to become a Pastor and gave him an exact prediction.

What she said was true. I guess that was a fair test. I agree Bob to become your sponsor."

Helena left the office to tell Lisette the good news. Bob just smiled at Grace as he walked by. "Aren't you going to congratulate me?" Grace was fuming but didn't dare say anything until she found out how Bob knew. She didn't trust him and planned to talk her mother out of letting Bob become active in their church.

Story

Chapter 17 – War Begins

Lottie was trying to find any excuse to receive Bob's attention. "The bathroom is so beautiful, Bob." She hugged him tight pretending the beauty of his work overwhelmed her. The truth was it was a fabulous job. Bob really did know how to make a masterpiece. He showed her little finishing touches he had added that really made the room stand out.

Trying to keep some control, Lottie said, "I understand we agreed on the price for the work. That was actually below market price so I'm willing to pay more if you like."

Bob said, "No. I do agree you would have spent at least another $1,000.00 for anyone else to do the work but we will call that room and board. I really hate imposing on you this long. With the money, I

MIA TENROC

should be able to find a room to rent and get out of your hair."

Panic rose inside of Lottie, "Even if you are working other jobs, why not rent the room here? It's clean, nice, and quiet. I can take pictures of your work and show them around. I bet I can find you other jobs."

Bob really wanted to leave but he thought of one more way to use Lottie. "I suppose for a while but not long. I like being independent. We can see what happens the next few weeks. I would appreciate the offer to look for other remodeling jobs. Lottie, I've been wanting to ask you for something." Lottie gazed at him looking hopeful. "I know you are a member of the church board. I've decided to become a Pastor. I want to be more active in the church. There is a board position that has opened up with one of the beloved members going into the spirit world last week. Do you think you could nominate me for the chair?"

Lottie looked surprised, "I would be glad to do so. I didn't realize how much interest you had in the church. Of course, with our schedules, we've had very little time to talk. Something you might want to think about is that most Pastors are better received when they are married. I do believe you might be able to get a church without a wife, especially with your talent in music."

73

FLAWED DECISIONS MURDER

Bob realized with his request he would have to continue to string Lottie along. "I realize this is in a sense your money but I would like to take you to dinner tonight to celebrate the completion of the job and the hope of the future." Lottie was thrilled.

The next morning, they went to church together. Helena called Bob into the office after the service. "Grace really doesn't believe you are right for a Pastor position. I admit I have the same reservations. I gave you my word to sponsor you, so what I decided was that we will continue with your training. I'm sure by the time you have completed the course, we will all know for certain that the life with this church is right for you. When it comes time to sign-off on the papers, if it doesn't feel right, well we will cross that bridge at that time. Does that sound fair to you?"

Bob turned on his charm, "Certainly it does. I have no doubt that you will consider me worthy of the position at that time." As Bob left the office, he noticed Grace hiding in the kitchen of the fellowship hall. He gave her a big smile proving that he wasn't worried about her interference.

In the car going home, Bob told Lottie what Helena had said. Lottie surprised him with good news. "There are a lot of people in the church that don't like Helena. She is controlling and vindictive. In case you didn't notice, the members of the church love Lisette.

MIA TENROC

She shows kindness and consideration to all. Helena is jealous of that and started not to sign-off on Lisette's final papers. The board called Helena in and wanted to know why she wouldn't let Lisette preach when she draws a larger crowd than Helena does. She made flimsy excuses about her sermons weren't smooth enough or she acted on impulse too much. We told her either she signs the papers or we would look for a new Senior Pastor. Needless to say, she signed and Lisette became an Associate Pastor. It has all worked out for the good of the church. Lisette shows love and respect for Helena. Some members avoid confiding in Helena, fearing she will somehow use their concerns against them. Thus, they will seek Lisette for counseling. I still see the envy in Helena about how much respect Lisette receives."

Bob asked, "How many on the board are pro-Lisette?"

Lottie said, "All of us think Lisette would be a great leader for the church."

Bob then asked, "How many are anti-Helena?"

Lottie thought, "There are 12 members on the board. Most of us realize Helena started this church, along with her sister. The decision about her actions often comes down to a 50/50 split."

Bob started to think of an even deeper plan to get his desire, should Helena get in his way.

Abletown

Chapter 18 – Missy

Fannie and Jean headed toward the hotel that Missy had turned into the other day. Jean said, "I just don't understand how people can be so determined to manipulate others. The story I am currently telling is about this guy tricking others into doing what he wants in a church. Missy wants to control Leon for some reason. Why would someone 20 years younger throw herself at a married man?"

Fannie laughed, "It's not like getting a mayor of a little town would be that big of a catch. Do you think Belinda is right about how much she was making a pass at Leon?"

Jean nodded yes, "I saw it for myself the other day. It's not something I'm willing to tell because gossip can spread fast and be mistaken for fact. I do

MIA TENROC

know that Leon walked away from her. Belinda texted that Missy hasn't show up at the campaign headquarters today so far. I wouldn't if I were her. I would be embarrassed at my actions. I want to know what she is after."

Fannie questioned, "What are we going to say to her? Do you have a plan?"

Jean said, "No, not really. I was just going to ask her directly why she was after Leon."

At the hotel, Jean and Fannie went to the registration desk. It was so dirty and sleazy that Jean felt her skin crawl. "Hello, I'm looking for someone that is living here." She showed a picture she snapped on her cell phone of Missy.

The guy glanced but didn't look much. "What do you want her for? My customers have a right to their privacy. Are you the police?"

Jean looked surprised. Nothing about her or Fannie shouted police. "No. Could you please buzz the woman and ask her to come to the lobby?"

The man rang a number and then hung up without saying anything. "No answer."

Jean explained, "I saw this woman walking down the street about 2:00 p.m. last Friday. Her purse was hanging open and an envelope fell out. I tried to shout to her but she didn't hear me. She got into her car and

FLAWED DECISIONS MURDER

drove off. I picked up the envelope and it had some things inside that I know she would want back. This address is inside so I thought it would be the right thing to do to bring it to her."

The man looked up and inspected the two ladies. "What kind of things?"

Jean continued to lie, "For one thing, it contains some money and other papers of importance."

The man gave a menacing smile, "She owes me back rent. Why don't you give it to me? I will pass it on to her with her debt paid to me."

Jean said, "No. She knows where she was last Friday. Tell her the envelope will be in that office if she wants it." The man went back to reading his paper and said no more.

Outside, Fannie saw a young woman about 20 years old. She was clearly dressed as a prostitute. "Excuse me. We are looking for this woman. Can you help us locate her?"

The girl looked at the picture and said, "I don't know why you would want her. She doesn't do women."

Jean and Fannie looked at each other in shock. Fannie replied, "Are you saying she is a lady of the evening?"

MIA TENROC

The girl looked offended. "What's wrong with that? It's her choice but like I said, she specializes in older men. Some older men want young girls like me because they are perverts. Some senior men are just looking for company and don't want to feel like they are doing their daughters. That's the kind she specializes in since she is in her mid-thirties. What kind of girl are you after? I was just headed to work but if you are interested…"

Jean blushed, "I'm so sorry that we didn't make ourselves clear. We aren't looking for that. This woman dropped an envelope the other day. Friday at 2:00 to be exact. We are just trying to return it."

The girl was bored with the conversation since there was no money in it for her. "Haven't seen her for a few days."

Jean said, "Please tell her that the envelope will be at the office outside where she dropped it."

The girl was a little curious now. "Exactly what office is that? She said that she has a big fish and wouldn't be on the corner for a while. I wouldn't mind a permanent gig either."

Fannie asked, "Did she say what the gig was? Did she say with whom?"

The girl walked away. "No. Quit wasting my time."

FLAWED DECISIONS MURDER

Fannie and Jean got back in the car. Fannie started laughing very hard. "We were mistaken as both police and perverts in just a few minutes. Do you think they will forget their conversation with us or did we older ladies give them a laugh? Hey, do you think I can earn more money here than running the store, since some guys want an older woman?"

Jean didn't even want to think about it. She wanted to get home and get a shower.

Abletown

Chapter 19 – The Date

The next morning, the ladies settled in on the porch of the Friend's Home except for Priscilla. Jean asked, "To whom did Priscilla make her excuse for not joining us today?"

Eve held up her arm, "That would be me. She said with working on Peter's campaign, she didn't have time to sit around. She is working at the Senior Center in the mornings and on the campaign in the afternoons."

Belinda said, "The other day I was going door-to-door, handing out brochures of what Leon stood for and answering any questions that the residents might have on his stances. Most of the time, people aren't home because they are working. In that case, we leave the information on the door handle saying to call

FLAWED DECISIONS MURDER

headquarters if they have any questions. I saw Priscilla doing the same thing on the other side of the street and crossed over to say hi. I told her which houses on the north side of the street didn't answer their doors. She gave me a dirty look and said they were probably home and just didn't want to talk to me. I can't believe how rude she was. Other than Priscilla, I have talked to a few hundred people in town. Most even invite me in to have tea and pie or cake. I've made friends with many people I never knew before. Besides the Leon campaign, I take time to ask if they have ideas that they would want our local charity foundation to sponsor. I heard some good projects for us to consider. I will bring it up at the next meeting."

Josephine said, "I got a letter from Priscilla that says the foundation meeting has been postponed and that she will let us know when it would be rescheduled. Money was left by Cassandra to be used for the good of the town. Even though Mrs. Reid named Priscilla as director, she made it very clear that all of us were to be on the board with the decisions that are made. I have a feeling that Priscilla is going to try to exclude us."

Jean wasn't interested in talking about Priscilla, "The terms of use for the money is very clear. Even if we weren't on the board, the money still has to be for the benefit of the town. Eve, what is on the back of

MIA TENROC

your hand? Did you get a tattoo? You really are into this biker thing."

Eve laughed, "I don't have the nerve to do a real tattoo. These are the water kind that children use. It washes off. I'm going riding on a motorcycle this afternoon and thought it looked more the part of a biker chick."

Everyone doubled over with laughter. Josephine said, "Are you going with the guy that stopped by the other night?"

Eve blushed, "That's the problem with living next door to your good friend. Yes, he is a policeman named Connor."

Jean had a shocked look on her face. "Don't you think you are playing with fire? You are married."

Eve defended herself, "We are just friends. We really hit it off. He is newly divorce and just wants someone to talk to. Nothing is happening. I know I am married but let's face it, Nigel lives on the farm with his junk and I live in town and work to pay for everything. He makes very little money by occasionally selling his collectables as he calls them. He doesn't want to sit and talk to me. Everything that goes wrong is my fault. I'm tired of hearing about how much I've changed in looks. Connor enjoys being with me and isn't critical of me. I'm enjoying

FLAWED DECISIONS MURDER

his company. I think I deserve a little happiness. I'm not doing anything wrong or to feel guilty about."

Jean said, "I apologize. It was none of my business. You are right that you deserve kindness and respect. I was just worried for you at the moment. Why don't we get back to our story and away from reality?"

Story

Chapter 20 – The Plan

Lottie reported to Bob. "I talked to the committee. They said you couldn't be on the board since you are employed by the church. They asked if I had any other suggestions for a new committee member. I said I would think about it and get back to them. Do you have any ideas of someone that might be a good fit?"

"I would think Violet would be a good fit." Bob realized he might have responded too quickly so he felt a need to justify his selection. "I never talked to her about it so I don't know if she has a pro-Helena point of view. I just choose her because she doesn't talk much but is always active in the church. There are times she is setting up the displays, working on the sign, or taking care of the flowers on the alter. I

FLAWED DECISIONS MURDER

think she shows an interest in the church but isn't too opinionated. Maybe you know her better than I do. What do you think of that idea?"

Lottie at first was ruffled by the suggestion but upon hearing his explanation, she realized Bob was really thinking of the church. "That is a good idea. I will talk to her at the service today. I don't want to nominate her if she is a fan of Helena. It's ok if she is respectful of her service. I want someone that knows right from wrong and does not blindly follow a leader."

Bob said, "One day, I heard her say she attended the church because of the diversity of the members. She liked the freedom to interpret the messages she heard from the altar without the church being in control of her thoughts or people being judgmental of her."

Lottie gave a snorting sound. "She doesn't know Helena well if she thinks that. Helena judges everyone."

Bob thought it was best to end the conversation there. "I don't know the other members well. Maybe you know of someone you think might be better. I just want to keep the church welcoming to all."

Lottie reached over and held his hand. "You are so considerate of others." Bob wanted to pull his hand away but fought off the impulse.

MIA TENROC

Bob went into the fellowship hall. Violet was working in the kitchen. "Hey, you good-looking young lady." Violet blushed but didn't say anything. "Did you know they needed a new committee member? I told Lottie I thought you would be good for the job."

Violet looked irritated. "I'm not interested in being on a committee. I don't want to be making the decisions here. I work hard all week long. This is my place to come and relax."

Bob smiled, "I'm playing with Lonny's group again next weekend. Why don't you come over and watch us? That would be relaxing and a lot of fun."

Violet looked around, "Lottie would kill us both if she heard you invited me. Will she be there?"

Bob glanced around and saw Lottie over across the room. "I don't let her know where I play because I don't want her to come. This isn't really a date. I just thought it would be fun and relaxing for you to have a night out."

Violet looked down shyly, "I guess it wouldn't hurt anything for me to give it a try."

Bob smiled at her and told her the time and location.

Lottie spotted them across the room and hurried over. "Violet, is Bob telling you about our great idea?

FLAWED DECISIONS MURDER

I think I will nominate you for the board of directors. Would you be interested?"

Violet shook her head no. "I'm not a leader. I'm just go to church to relax from the busy week."

Lottie grabbed her hand. "That's why you would be ideal. You would provide common sense advice. We only meet once a month unless there is an emergency. I know this might be a sudden surprise, so why don't you think about it and get back to me later?"

Violet promised she would but in reality, she had already made up her mind to say no.

Story

Chapter 21 – Relaxing

Violet entered the bar where the band was going to play. She noticed that she didn't feel relaxed at all. The fear of Lottie finding out she was there to watch Bob and the lack of understanding of Bob's intentions made her very nervous.

Bob turned from plugging in his guitar into the sound board to see her enter. The smile he gave was genuine. "I'm so glad you came. I want you to be honest about my performance tonight. The other girlfriends and wives are sitting in that booth over there. Why don't I go introduce you so you don't have to sit alone? I like to go outside on my breaks to get fresh air. Maybe you can join me then."

FLAWED DECISIONS MURDER

Violet was introduced as a friend from church to the other ladies. They were very nice and welcomed her to the table. "What kind of church do you go to?"

Violet tried to think how to describe it so that it would make sense. "It is a Spiritual Church. We talk to the spirits of people that passed before us." The ladies looked at her weird. Violet tried to explain, "It's for people that don't fit into a conventional church. As a Native American, we do believe in the Spirit World so I kind of fit in there to a degree."

The conversation changed to the bar and the music to be played. Violet didn't add much but listened a lot. She was glad not to be the center of attention. The music was very good and she did start to relax a little. She and Bob chatted during the breaks but nothing special was said.

After the evening was over, Violet was very tired. She never went out at night. Bob suggested, "Why don't we stop and get a bite to eat? My treat. I need to unwind before I can sleep at night." Violet went along because she was not one to raise objections. Besides, she liked Bob's company.

After settling in and ordering, Bob asked, "Tell me about your business. The cream you gave me the other day worked really good."

This was a subject that Violet was comfortable with. "Nature gives us all the medicines we need. If

MIA TENROC

you are out in the hot sun, there are certain trees that you can rub the bark and a white powdery substance will come off on your hand. Rub that powder over your body and it will act as suntan lotion. There are always vines that grow together. If you get poison ivy, there will be a vine growing nearby that you can make into a tea to drink that cures it. Natural remedies don't cause the negative side effects that drugs do. I told you once before, my father is a medicine man. He is so knowledgeable about plants and herbs. Our people relied on them for years to stay healthy. There is a trend now that people want to use natural products instead of the medication their doctors prescribe. Our business has had a fifty percent increase in the past two years. My father tries to teach me but I don't think I will ever know everything he does."

Bob was very interested. "You understand that I'm changing a lot of things in my life. I have an interest to become a Pastor in the church to reach the Spirit World. I also have a big interest in learning about the medicines you are talking about. I'm trying to be more in one with nature and the world. Would you be interested in teaching me more? I would really like to meet your father someday."

Violet felt a kinship with Bob right then. "I'm sure my father would like to meet you too. If you have some spare time, you are welcome to come by the store and I will explain more about the products."

FLAWED DECISIONS MURDER

Bob reached out and took her hand. He didn't say anything for a long time. "You have such an inner peace. I enjoy being with you." He was sincere but he also was thinking about the increase in business. He was going to check out the business model and see if there was enough money to support him comfortably. He wanted to move out from Lottie as soon as possible and he really did like being with Violet. "What about your mother? You never speak of her."

Violet looked depressed, "My mother died in childbirth. I never knew her but I blame myself for her death. My father has always been protective of me and a wonderful parent. He doesn't blame me, but I do. I wish I had known her. Father loved her very much. He chooses to never marry again. In our culture, we are named after something in nature that we see when exiting the birthing hut. Father saw a patch of violets and so that is my name. His mother saw an eagle soaring and that became his name, Soaring Eagle. He always tells me that the eagle only mates once in life and if that mate dies, the eagle lives alone. He is following his namesake. You aren't permitted to call him by this native name. Only tribe members and family can. That is why to you he will introduce himself as Grey."

Abletown

Chapter 22 – Mating

That portion of the story made Eve laugh. "I've been married five times to four different men. I would have to be named after an animal that mated plenty. I've never been able to find the right guy."

Josephine looked curious. "How did you do that?"

Eve explained, "Number two and number four was the same man. I didn't learn my lesson the first time, I guess. Besides number three, was so bad that it made number two look great."

Belinda smiled, "Do you have a number six on the horizon?"

Eve answered with a chuckle, "I don't cheat on my husbands. That is why I leave them if I become

FLAWED DECISIONS MURDER

interested in someone new. I really love being with Connor but right now I don't see myself marrying him. He is a lot younger than I am. I know he still wants to have a family and I'm definitely not the right person for that. I could fix him up with my daughter, I guess. It would be a relief to find her someone that would keep her in line. I'm not trying to lead Connor on. We're just friends. I think of myself as more of a confidant."

Since Priscilla had an excuse not to show up again, the others felt free to talk. Jean told them about her and Fannie's attempt to find out what Missy was doing hanging out with Leon. The others got a good laugh. Belinda suggested, "Why don't we head over to Fannie's Attic so we can hear her perspective of the trip?"

When they entered, they found Fannie dressed from clothes in the costume rental section of the store. She had her hair teased out, a lot of make-up, dressed in pantaloons, a white peasant blouse and a corset over top. Jean shouted, "Good golly, you are a sight! The store is open right now. You need to put some clothes on."

Fannie stood in front of a full-length mirror and ran her hand along her waistline and over her hips. "Do you think an older man might pick me up in this?"

94

MIA TENROC

Belinda used logic, "I guess if he had a pill to help him out, that an 80-year-old man might get turned on?"

Fannie was offended, "What about someone with a mother fetish?"

Josephine went over with a robe, "Beauty is in the eye of the beholder. Not everyone entering in the store might want to behold. You are still attractive but there is no R-rated sign on the store front so children might be damaged for life if they entered."

Even more irked, Fannie responded, "I have more on than most people you will see at a swimming pool. Besides, steam punk is in and I think I fit the bill for that."

Josephine removed the robe from her shoulders. "Your right. Go for it." As the others laughed, she questioned, "Why would you want someone younger? Do you really want to have a boytoy?"

Fannie thought about it and then put on a skirt over the bottom, making it an odd but acceptable outfit. "I guess I better not think of the other profession. Did you tell them what happened? Jean was so embarrassed. You should have seen her face. I haven't figured out why a prostitute would want to work on a political campaign."

FLAWED DECISIONS MURDER

Jean felt she knew that answer. "My guess is to discredit him. Peter could always say something like, 'look at the type of people helping Leon?' Belinda saw Missy flirting with Leon. If he took her up on it, she could kiss and tell."

Belinda said, "I was so glad she didn't come back to the office. I hope she stays away. I talked to Leon and told him I thought it would be best for her not to help. Leon agreed that if she shows up again, he will ask her to leave."

Josephine pondered, "Did he ever call her? You wouldn't want his number to appear on her cell phone."

Belinda shuddered, "I'm afraid it already is on there. He thought she was so great and I know he called to ask her advice a couple of times."

Jean said, "When we were leaving the hotel the other day, I told Fannie that it could come back to haunt us. I don't doubt that the calls to her phone could haunt him as well."

Belinda suggested, "I'm thinking a proactive marketing approach might be necessary. I could point out how he treats everyone respectfully and will return any calls made to him, no matter who they are."

Abletown

Chapter 23 – Friendship Splits

Mr. Manor entered the store. His expression showed that he thought Fannie's outfit was unusual. "I hope I'm not interrupting anything. I was wondering if I could talk to you ladies."

Jean answered, "No, you haven't interrupted a thing. This is just a normal day of chatting over tea, with Fannie being her usual Bohemian self."

Mr. Manor glanced around the store, "Are we alone?"

Fannie assured him, "This store doesn't exactly attract a large crowd, especially during Jean's tea time. Feel free to talk. If someone comes in, we can change the subject if you like."

FLAWED DECISIONS MURDER

Mr. Manor looked embarrassed. "I might be unprofessional here but I have a major concern. Jean, Fannie, Eve, Josephine and Belinda, you are all on the board of Mrs. Reid's trust. The purpose of the trust was to make Abletown a better place to live. It is to help the citizens of this town achieve more happiness and success."

Belinda said, "We are aware of the purpose that Mrs. Reid wanted. I certainly hope we are living up to her expectations."

Mr. Manor blushed, "You do perform the tasks of board members very well. Priscilla came to me the other day and wanted to donate money to Peter's campaign. I told her that the money could not be spent without the approval of the board, which are you ladies. Mrs. Reid chose Priscilla as head trustee due to their close friendship. However, she was also well aware that Priscilla was not a leader. Belinda and Eve, we know it was your efforts that improved the book collection at the library. Jean and Josephine, you two led the restoration project of the old cemetery. Mrs. Reid was worried that if she chose either Jean, Belinda or someone else, that it would hurt Priscilla's feelings. That is why she made the safeguard of appointing all of you, the real leaders of Abletown, to the board to make the final decisions. I told Priscilla we needed to have a board meeting to approve the campaign donation. Not only did she refuse but she also canceled the upcoming meeting already scheduled. Can you please tell me what is going on? Why is Priscilla acting so oddly?"

Josephine took up the challenge of explaining, "I will answer because Jean will be reluctant to say something negative about Priscilla. Belinda is working for Leon's campaign and when Priscilla found out, she got very upset. Priscilla went and volunteered for Peter's campaign that very day. Jean has also expressed her support for Leon. Since then, Priscilla quit working out with us and avoided the tea and porch time talks. She has a right to vote for whomever she wants and we respect that. We all agreed not to mention the mayor election again, but Priscilla has a way of overreacting. I can tell you that no matter who I plan to support for mayor, my vote would be no to any campaign contributions. I don't believe it fits in with Mrs. Reid's plan to improve the town. We are a small town of about 1,500 people. We give multiple opportunities for the candidates to debate the issues. They can get their ideas and messages out by walking around the town and speaking to people. The newspaper gives each candidate so many words a week to express themselves. Those columns in the newspaper are exactly the same size, on the same page, and without any commentary from the owners of the newspaper. I reiterate that my vote will be no."

FLAWED DECISIONS MURDER

Eve took up the conversation, "Why don't we do a vote right now? All in favor of a donation, raise your hand." No one moved. "All against donations, raise your hand." All hands went up, including Belinda and Jean. "Looks like you have our vote. I suppose now, Priscilla wants to replace us as board members."

Mr. Manor's mouth opened but there was a pause before the words came out, "It has been mentioned. This is a really hard position for me to be in. If I tell you too much, would I be breaking a confidence? As board members, you have a right to know what is going on."

Jean asked in a quiet voice, "What are the rules or guidelines for voting to get a board member off? What are the rules for a no-confidence vote on the trustee of the charity? I don't think we should do anything yet. The election will be in a few weeks, and this might all blow over after that. If it doesn't, I question if we will be able to work together for the best interest of the trust."

Mr. Manor had come prepared, "I have a copy of the trust, which was recorded in the official records due to the transfer of title of Mrs. Reid's home. I highlighted the area that applies to voting in and out of the various officers. This is something I never

MIA TENROC

thought would be needed unless someone passed away. This whole event is most upsetting."

After Mr. Manor left, Jean suggested to everyone, "Let's continue the story during water aerobics this afternoon to distract ourselves of this incident."

Story

Chapter 24 – Violet

Violet was speaking on the phone to her father who was in Oklahoma. "Father, I'm not interested in Bob, but it is nice to have someone to go out with at night so I'm not sitting home alone. I don't plan for him to move in with me. I was just expressing my concern for him living at Lottie's because I don't trust her."

"Take care, my daughter. If this woman is as unbalanced as you say, she might consider you a threat. Why don't you offer her my calming spray? It should create a more positive attitude in the house if she uses it."

Violet promised she would offer the spray as a gift, and that she would be careful to only display friendship with Bob.

MIA TENROC

At church that weekend, Violet gave a gift bag to Lottie. "Thank you, Violet. I'm so surprised by your kind offer of a gift. I just don't understand why. It's not my birthday or a holiday."

Violet tried to smile, "Sometimes you just get moved to do something kind for someone. I was looking at the spray in the store and thought with the positive energy it gives off, that you might find it relaxing to spray in your home. I use it in mine. There doesn't need to be a reason for an act of friendship."

Lottie gave Violet a hug. "Again, thank you. By the way, did you think any more about the committee position we discussed? I understand you said no and really were sincere about it, but I think you are a leader in a quiet way. You lead more by example than by what you say. I think you would be perfect for the job. You would listen to everyone else and then express your opinion in such a way that people would listen to logic."

Violet shook her head no again. "It's just not me. I would only do it if I felt a special calling."

Bob was hiding in the broom closet overhearing the conversation. Those that would be visited by spirits on the stage either hid in the closet or in the kitchen of the fellowship hall where they could see and overhear the other members talk and get ideas to use for when they pretended the spirits visited them.

103

FLAWED DECISIONS MURDER

He knew Richard was hiding in the kitchen listening as well.

When the members of the church went in for the healing portion of the service, Bob went over to talk to Richard in the kitchen. "Richard, did you hear what Violet and Lottie were saying? I agree with Lottie and think Violet would make a great board member. What do you think?"

Richard replied, "I also heard Lisette talk about that. I don't know why she decided Violet was the person for the job, but I know she would like it."

Bob continued to manipulate, "I think one of us should give Violet the special calling. Do you want to do so? I would but I was the one to suggest it to Lottie. I was with Lottie when it was suggested to Violet. If I have a spirit visit to give her that message, she might think it was contrived."

Richard gave Bob a puzzled look, "Isn't that what we are doing with this conversation?"

Bob retorted, "Isn't that what we do with the entire service?"

Richard inquired, "If you don't truly believe in spirits, why do you want to be a Pastor?"

"I think some people can talk with spirits, and I hope to become one of them. I believe Lisette does, don't you?"

MIA TENROC

Richard nodded yes, "My wife has a great many gifts. I admit to going along with doing this spirit delivery thing to try to fool her into thinking I have the gift too. I guess that is wrong and I'm not being a good husband by doing so. I love her so much; I would do anything to make sure we are on the same wavelength."

Bob was feeling guilty because of his lust for Lisette. He put his hand on Richard's shoulder and said with sincerity, "Richard, you are a good man and a good husband. I would do the same thing in your shoes. I agree you have a fine woman. I wish you the best with her." The words were genuine but he wished he was in those shoes.

The two men went up on the stage. Bob delivered the first message to a couple he overheard bragging that they were going to be grandparents. "You two in the second row. Yes, you. I see you are going to have a new experience. Something bright and happy will be happening to you in the near future. I keep getting the word 'bundle'. That that mean anything to you?"

Surprised, the woman replied, "How amazing! Yes, we just found out we will be grandparents. You are probably hearing bundle of joy."

Bob smiled and said, "You're right. I see it clearly now. You will be enjoying a little one."

FLAWED DECISIONS MURDER

Richard got up and described the spirit he saw, "You, young man in the back to the right. We don't know each other, correct?" The man shook his head no. Richard continued, "I see a bright future for you, too. This one involves books. Did you apply at a university recently?" The man shook his head yes. "I believe the spirits are saying you will have a favorable response."

Richard and Bob traded time giving a few more predictions. When Richard was on his last turn, he pointed to Violet. "This time, a spirit has come to me. She is a woman in her 20's when she died. I never saw a picture of your mother but she looks a lot like you. She wants you to be a leader. I don't know what leadership she is implying. It might be in business or for a club or even here at the church. She says to lead when it presents itself." Violet just sat there blushing.

After the service, Violet went to Lottie. "I believe my mother wants me to accept the committee position so if you nominate me, I will accept."

Lottie gave her a hug. "You are full of surprises today. I think you will be perfect. I am proud to nominate you."

Bob could overhear the entire conversation and smiled at his accomplishment. If that hateful Helena wasn't going to sign the paperwork to make him a pastor, he would use the board to remove her as an obstacle in his way.

Story

Chapter 25 – Accounting

Lottie was thrilled when Violet was sworn in to be on the board that governed the church. "I'm sure we made the right decision in confirming Violet to be one of us. Violet, we have twelve members and in case of a tie, the head Pastor makes the deciding vote. When I call on people, it is by their chair number. Being the newest member, I will refer to you as chair #12. Everyone has their numbers in front of where they sit. This church is growing steadily. As the committee chairwoman for this year, I propose setting down the goals that this church should accomplish. Does anyone have any suggestions or input on this? I recognize chair #5. Please contribute."

Chair #5 spoke, "I think we need to be more noticeable in the community. I suggest we put on a festival with games and prizes for the children. We can do spiritual messages and palm readings for the adults."

Lottie replied, "Excellent idea! All in favor, say 'Yea'. The entire group agrees but I need to ask: are they any 'Nay'?" No one objected. "Chair #5, Joan, would you like to head the committee for the festival?" Joan nodded yes. "Great! I appreciate that. I suggest you ask members of the church to volunteer and when you select a date, submit it for approval and we will add it to the church calendar. We are here to help you but will only do so if you request it. We trust you to be in full control, without interference from the committee."

Chair #7 raised his hand and was recognized by Lottie. "I think to set the budget and spending plan for next year, we need to see the accounting records. I know we have been given a bottom-line sheet with the balance each month. I think it is our responsibility that the money spent is in accordance with the budget we set."

Helena spoke in an offended voice. "The bills are all paid! We have no major expenses since my sister owned and dedicated this building free of charge to be used as a church. You have a statement of the balance of each account. What are you wanting? Do you expect to see every check written? I assure you my

FLAWED DECISIONS MURDER

daughter, our volunteer accountant, does the committees' bidding."

Chair #7 replied, "I'm not saying anything bad about your daughter. I've known Grace since she was a little girl. I just feel that since the number of people attending has doubled in the last five years that we need to have more of a check and balance system in place. Membership rolls have shown a fifty percent increase in people attending the church. It seems odd that the balances in the accounts have only grown by twenty percent. Do you think that the long-time members are donating less? Or are the new members not donating their fair share? Have our utilities or other expenses in the church increased a lot? I just think this committee is responsible to making sure that contributions are wisely spent."

Helena's anger was increasing as her cheeks turned red, "I will have Grace give a more detailed report to the committee for next month and let's see if that takes care of your concerns. She can list donations, expenses, and balances."

Lottie, wanting to keep the peace, suggested, "Why don't Grace and you, Helena, come up with a new style of report that we can review next month. We can vote then on approving the new report or suggest changes. We can do the budget on the monthly income we used last year, then if we receive

110

MIA TENROC

more, we can decide if it should stay in the bank or be spent on special purchases or expenses. It's best to plan on less income and get more. Does anyone else have any other matters we need to discuss this month? Good. Does anyone want to conclude the meeting? Thank you, Chair #8. Can I get a second? Thank you, chair #2. Meeting adjourned."

Lottie invited Violet to stop for coffee on the way home. Violet was really tired but didn't want to appear rude so she agreed to do so. Lottie explained, "I just wanted to take time to thank you again for taking the church position. I think new blood is important because they can bring new ideas."

Violet asked, "It seems that Chair #7 has concerns over the money situation. Is there anything I should know?"

Lottie tried to act reluctant, "Chair #7 stated he placed cash in the offering plate and didn't get credit for it on the list of donations. He needed the credit to use for his tax deduction. He claims, behind Helena's back, that he saw Grace spend that bill at a grocery store the next day. He knew it was the one he put in because he wrote his name on it. He wants to make sure Grace is being honest. Using his position on the committee, he can accomplish that without making a possibly false accusation."

FLAWED DECISIONS MURDER

Violet thought, "I hope I didn't get myself into something negative."

Abletown

Chapter 26 – Eve's Report

Since Jean had asked Eve to spy in Peter's campaign office to spot any irregularities, Eve invited Jean over for a glass of wine one evening to discuss her findings. "Peter asked me to help with the accounting since that is my profession. I work on his books for the city and for some personal businesses. He trusts me and should know I would never permit any funny business."

Jean surmised, "I take it you have found something questionable, otherwise you wouldn't be talking to me in private."

Eve laughed, "You're no fun. It like you read people's minds sometimes. You're right. I do have a couple of things that bother me."

FLAWED DECISIONS MURDER

Jean smiled, "It's logic, not mind reading. Be glad you weren't my child because you don't have a poker face and are easy to read."

Eve continued, "The campaign is paying a woman named Trudy Must as a private consultant. I asked about her and Peter said there is no need for the rest of us to meet with her. Peter says he talks to her and decides which of her suggestions he will take. The checks for Trudy are listed in the books without her name, only the word 'consultant'. They are always made payable to cash, they are taken to the bank, and a money order is obtained. I have no receipt of the money orders or an address where they are mailed. The second thing I don't like is he pays a photographer a large amount of money to follow him around and take pictures. He says it is for campaign literature and for newspapers to use. After the first pamphlets were sent out, why would he need more? Also, the newspaper uses their own photographer. It seems like a waste of money and he pays a very high price. Again, the checks labeled photographer are payable to cash, Peter takes them to the bank, and obtains money orders. The third thing I don't like is some campaign contributions are made by a company that isn't even registered with the state as an existing business. The fourth thing is payments are being make to a printing company for the brochures that is about four times what it should cost. I don't know if he is doing something wrong or if he just doesn't know the value of certain services."

Jean was in thought. "I'll look into this Trudy Must person. The name sounds fake. Do you have the photographer's name?"

Eve said, "I only know Trudy's name because Peter mentioned it. I don't know the name of the photographer."

Jean suggested, "Why don't you give me the name of the printing company as well. You said the contribution comes from a non-registered company. How are the payments to the campaign made? Do they use a check, cashier check, or cash?"

Eve had that answer ready. "They come in monthly by money orders. The kind you buy at most gas stations or check-cashing companies. The name is so scribbled you can't tell what the name really is. Any idea if you think this stuff is legal or not?"

Jean replied, "Not without investigating it a lot further. I doubt Peter would do something illegal and get himself in trouble. I don't believe he is a bad man. He doesn't realize how the modernization and destruction of these beautiful old homes would ruin the antique business this town is famous for. I don't believe he realizes the expense of upgrading the sewer, electrical system, roads, and schools. Are you planning to vote for him?"

FLAWED DECISIONS MURDER

Eve answered, "I'm still on the fence. I am good friends with Peter and his wife, but I don't agree with all of his ideas. I'm trying to encourage him to find a balance between what the builders want and what is best for the current residents of the town. I feel like he listens to me but there has been no change in his policies at this point. I guess I'm more of a wait-and-see type person. Priscilla occasionally talks to me but feels like I'm betraying Peter by doing the workouts with you and Belinda. She acts like you are the enemy instead of someone with a different opinion."

Jean was irritated, "That is her choice. I get tired of her making excuses not to visit or work out with us. Why send messages through you and Josephine? She should just be honest and say she is choosing not to be with us any longer. I have been thinking long and hard about if I should resign from the committee that oversees Mrs. Reid's trust. It's not like we profit from the money personally and it takes our time. I'm considering just handing Priscilla that victory."

Eve responded, "On the one hand, I agree with you but on the other hand, we promised Mrs. Reid we would be there to help."

Jean changed the subject, "Is the tattoo by your ankle another water kind or did you get a real one?"

MIA TENROC

"Water, of course. I don't want the pain of needles for a real one. Do I look more like a biker chick with it?"

Abletown

Chapter 27 – The Body

Nick and his partner, Janice, were called to a crime scene on Thursday morning. On arrival, the officer that phones in stated, "We have a woman, white, mid-thirties, about 5 foot 6, guessing about 130 pounds, that was in the driver seat of the car. It appears she lost control of the car and drove into the lake. The car is about to be lifted out now. It looks like it had been in the water for a few days."

Nick and Janice walked to the edge of the lake to watch the tow truck pulling out the car. Janice noted, "No dents on the bumper or rear like she was forced off the road." She turned to the officer, "Who reported the accident?"

"Those kids were playing in the lake, throwing rocks and skipping stones. They heard a weird sound

MIA TENROC

like the rock had hit metal. You know like a 'ping' instead of a 'plop'. They waded into the water and discovered the car. One dived down, looked, and saw the body."

Nick walked over to speak to the boys, "Are you doing ok? It's kind of surprising to find a body."

The boy replied, "I'm weirded out some, but it's also kind of a cool story since I bet no one else in school ever had this experience. She didn't have any clothes on, you know."

Nick looked surprised, "I haven't got to see the body yet so no, I didn't know."

The boy continued, "I better leave that part out when I tell my mother. Do you think it will be in the newspaper?"

Nick looked over at the small group of reporters standing near the road. "I'm sure it will be so I would be totally honest with your mom. You did a brave thing, diving to look if you could help. It's not your fault she didn't have clothes on so I'm sure you won't get in trouble. Did you see anyone around today when you went to check on the car?" The boys all shook their heads no. "I noticed the tire marks in the grass. Do you boys come here every day? Did you notice the tire marks today or any other day?"

FLAWED DECISIONS MURDER

Another boy answered, "We haven't been here for a few days, but yeah, there were tire marks here on Monday when we came over."

The first boy said, "You know how when you see dead bodies on the tv or movies underwater, they look like they are pretty and could almost be alive? The body was really gross. It was all bloated."

Nick said, "What you saw is reality. It's often not very nice to look at no matter where we find the body. Have you even seen the woman before today?" The boy shook his head no.

Their parents arrived and were kept on the street. Nick verified with the patrolman that he had the names and addresses of the youngsters. Nick walked the boys to their parents and praised them for being brave and good citizens for reporting the accident.

Janice laughed as Nick came over to her, "I didn't hear many words, only a lot of head nodding."

Nick smiled, "No one realizes the shock of a body, especially one in water, until they see it for themselves." He looked into the car. "Looks like one of her high heels was used to keep the gas pedal down. Do you see the odd way the shoe is jammed in there? I think we have a murder here."

The crime lab group was busy taking pictures of everything. The coroner arrived to take the body in for examination. The car was being towed to the crime lab. Nick and Janice not only made sure that everything was being handled properly but also looked for any other clues.

Janice said, "My bet is that the car was stopped on the road, aimed for the lake, the shoe was placed and the car came down without the guilty party setting foot on the grassy area. There was no attempt to apply the brakes or it would have shown up in the grass. I notice the watch on her wrist stopped at 2:00 p.m. It would've been daylight but there is no direct view from a house to this area. I guess we need to go interview the neighbors to see if someone noticed anything. I doubt if there will be much success."

Nick noticed, "I don't see any purse or registration in the car. I will run the plates. Hopefully, that will help us find out who she was. It looks like she was murdered elsewhere and this was staged."

Story

Chapter 28 – The Audit

"These books look like they are staged," said the accountant the committee hired to review the church records. "I'm not saying the figures aren't correct but every time someone sits down to write, the pressure on the pen, the flow of the ink, even the way the numbers are written can change if the person was tense or in a hurry. Many of these pages were clearly written on the same day, even though the information is over a few years in time."

Grace looked pale but was standing firm, "You are correct. Some days when I write, it is very sloppy. Since the books were going to be viewed by someone else, I went in and re-wrote the sloppy ones."

The accountant looked puzzled, "I realize this is a small business operation but why aren't you using an

MIA TENROC

accounting software system? There are many named ones out there that are very inexpensive. An accounting program would automatically calculate your total figures and save you time. Anyone authorized would be able to access it and review the records without having to pull out the physical books."

As head chairperson, Lottie responded, "We will research that and make a motion to discuss the change at another meeting. Is there anything else to disclose from your review?"

The accountant continued, "The reconciliation of the bank statements doesn't always match the entries in the books. You can see on this page in the books that there was a check written for $1,000.00 to Grace and then a deposit made by her for $1,000.00 back in the same month. However, the bank statements show that very deposit being made on the fourth of the next month."

Helena was getting angry, "Do you always remember what day it is when you are writing a check? Grace just confused the date since it is hand written. Let's get to the bottom line: are the books in balance or not?"

"Yes, if you take the past three years and don't look at the date of entries or how they match reports provided to this committee, the books are in balance

123

FLAWED DECISIONS MURDER

as of this date." The accountant was staring hard at Helena. "I will not say this is the best bookkeeping. There are discrepancies throughout the whole three years but at this point in time, the figures match. If you were to use a software system like I suggested, it would solve the dating errors. I also suggest that you have two people reconcile the bank statements instead of just one. I recommend that a member of this committee and the bookkeeper work in unison in providing the final reports provided to this committee and the congregation." He could tell that Grace was taking money on a regular basis. The check deposited by Grace was from Helena's checking account so her mother must be bailing her out. To say this fact aloud could set himself up for a slander suit so he concentrated on convincing the commitment to check and see for themselves.

Grace stood crying, "I have tried to serve this church for years. If you don't believe me to be a good and honest person then I will resign. I don't see any of you offering to help count the collections and spend your time doing the posting. It's a lot of hours I am giving in service to this church."

Lottie placed her arm around Grace's shoulders. "Please don't cry. No one is accusing you of being dishonest. I didn't realize how many hours you put in. From now on, we will be there to help with the various steps."

MIA TENROC

Grace realized this was not what she wanted. She regularly used the church money when she needed it. Being monitored would kill that flexibility. "I wasn't complaining. I don't mind the work at all. I just don't like being falsely accused, that's all."

Lottie turned to the accountant. "Thank you for checking the books and the suggestions for improvement. I will make sure we discuss the implementation of some or all of those ideas." She handed him a check for his services and walked him to his car. When she shook his hand to say thank you again, she turned so her face wouldn't be seen by someone looking out the window. "I got your hints in there. I'm smart enough to know why you can't say more than what you did. I'm working on the assumption that Grace isn't doing a good job and Helena has been covering up for her."

The accountant smiled, "You are a very smart woman."

Lottie couldn't wait to share the news with Bob. The discussion on the meetings were supposed to stay secret but this would add to his desire to oust Helena from the church. She thought if Bob did become a Pastor, then it would be better in appearance for him to have a wife. A rich wife would be an asset.

125

Story

Chapter 29 – Sermon Review

At this stage of his training, Bob needed to perform his first sermon. He asked Lisette to meet him at the church. "As you know, I will be preaching for the first time this Sunday. I feel Helena is working hard to prevent me from achieving my dream of becoming a Pastor. Every paper I submit to her for her opinion, she finds inadequate. I rework the papers to suit her preferences and turn them in to the online teacher. Then when I get back my papers, the criticisms I receive from the teacher always involve the portions that Helena required me to correct. I think she is deliberately giving me bad advice to make me look bad."

MIA TENROC

Lisette looked caringly at Bob. "It is so good you have this passion to improve your life. I would hate to think Helena would do something so nasty."

Bob tried to look sad to hide the anger he felt inside toward Helena. "I wrote my sermon. I was wondering if you could read it. I really want to do a good job. Your sermons are always so inspirational that I value your opinion."

Lisette read quietly without comment until she was done. "This is so great. I wouldn't change a thing. You really have a way of writing and talking with people that holds their attention. Richard agreed to record your sermon and upload it to the training site. I'm sure you will get a good grade. You haven't spoken about your son lately. How is he doing?"

Bob remembered the day he first met Lisette and longed for the hugging again. "Not too good, I'm afraid. I'm staying strong for him. I might take off in a few weeks and go up for a visit."

Lisette responded as Bob hoped. She came around the desk and gave him a hug. Bob was enjoying the embrace when he looked up and saw Richard standing in the doorway looking very disturbed. Bob reached out and said, "Please, come here Richard. Lisette just reviewed my sermon and said you would upload it for me." Richard walked over and Bob made sure to hug him as much as he just

FLAWED DECISIONS MURDER

hugged Lisette. "You both have been such good friends. I don't know what I would have done without you. As the wonderful couple you are, the work of this church is in good hands. I just told Lisette that my son isn't doing too good so I'm thinking of going up for a little bit."

Richard was very uncomfortable with the hug. He originally thought Bob was making excuses to get support from Lisette. For a brief moment, he had a slight bit of doubt. He broke Bob's embrace and hugged his wife. "Bob's right. You are so great. I do try my best to support you in all your efforts." With his arm around his wife, Richard turned to Bob. "I hope you get your Pastor's license. I will do all I can to help you. It would be so great to see you get your own church and to further our good works."

Richard and Lisette left to go to lunch. Bob remained for his appointment with Helena. After she read his sermon, the attacks began. "I think you have an understanding of the principle you plan to preach on. Here, let me make some suggested changes." Helena wrote on the paper the changes she wanted done. She knew that was one of the best sermons she had ever read. She wasn't smart enough to realize that helping Bob get his license might get him out of her church. No, she wanted him to fail.

MIA TENROC

Bob politely said, "I will take this home and review your suggestions. I will try to deliver a great sermon on Sunday." Bob walked away smiling.

Story

Chapter 30 – Delivery

Bob sat in the office reviewing his notes, while other people were starting the service. They performed the usual routine: false prophecies, pretend healing, and Lisette leading songs. Bob loved hearing that beautiful voice. Richard popped his head in the office and said, "It's time. Are you ready?"

Bob answered, "Please tell me you are ready to tape and upload the sermon."

Knowing that if Bob became a Pastor, he would likely leave their church, Richard was all too willing to help. "All is ready, but I have done one better for you. The sermon is being streamed live and Lisette talked your teacher into watching."

MIA TENROC

Panic came over Bob's face. "No pressure, right? Everything hangs on this now. Actually, that was a wise decision, that way Helena can't come and stop you from uploading the video."

Richard shook his head knowingly. "I know what you are about to do. Lisette told me about your conversation last night. We came up with this idea in order to avoid the fight we would have with Helena."

Bob walked onto the stage, turned to the small group of members and smiled. He stared at Helena for a moment, walked to the podium, and began to deliver his unaltered sermon. He didn't look at Helena again, choosing instead to meet eyes with Violet, Lisette, and Lottie, his support team. The satisfaction of defiance caused Bob to get more and more powerful in his delivery. He could hear comments of agreement coming from the audience. Bob's guitar sat on the stage. When the sermon was completed, he reached for the guitar and began to sing a song that supported his delivered words. The members actually applauded when he completed his show. He looked over to see Helena sitting like a rock. She didn't smile, didn't react, just starred in anger.

She came to him during fellowship time and ordered, "To my office, now!" Once inside, she yelled, "I will never sign off on you becoming a Pastor. How dare you disregard my advice!" Helena

131

FLAWED DECISIONS MURDER

held up the camera that Richard had used. "You are a disgrace! I want you to know that I deleted this contemptible act!"

Bob stood and towered over Helena. His wrathful glare was equal to hers. "You are a disgrace to this religion. You use your office to control others. People talk to Lisette, not you, because when people try to confide in you, they know it will be used against them. Your criticism on my work was intentionally used to make me fail. You will be your own undoing!"

Helena yelled, "You are fired from your job! You are never to darken these doors with your presence again!"

Bob smiled as he turned to leave. The crowd outside the door obviously overheard every word. He turned and said quietly, "I would expect an emergency meeting for the Board of Directors soon."

Bob was sitting with the comforting words and support of Lottie over dinner when the call came from his instructor. "What is going on over there?" she asked. "I just got a call from Helena saying you were no good and that she would never sign for you to become a Pastor. She said the sermon you delivered was a disaster. I told Helena that the sermon was broadcast live on our website today and that I loved it. I also informed her that we got calls from many of our members across the country praising it. She was totally surprised and seemed to have no knowledge about the steaming. Lisette hinted that she felt Helena disliked you so much that she couldn't be a good judge of your efforts. Do you feel that Helena is attempting to make you fail?"

Bob replied, "Yes. In order to prove to you that my work was better than what I previously turned in, I emailed you my original drafts with the changes made in Helena's handwriting. I know it will be a lot more work for you, but could you please reread my papers so you will be judging my actual work? Do you think I'm unfit or failed to understand what is right to present as a Pastor of this church?"

His instructor remained quiet for a few minutes then responded, "I need to consider all that I have learned. I can't sign off on you to be a Pastor due to our rules, but there are ways to work around Helena. I need to meet with the National Council for instructions on how to proceed. I will be back with you. This isn't over yet. I recommend you avoid Helena until you hear from me."

Lottie overheard the whole conversation. "I think we need an emergency meeting with our Board of Directors to have a confidence vote on Helena. After the show today, I think we can get enough votes to accomplish that."

FLAWED DECISIONS MURDER

Bob gave Lottie a hug. "You are such a friend and supporter. My concern is for Lisette and Richard. Now that Helena knows about the streaming, she will know Richard did the act and might try to get revenge."

Lottie looked surprised, "I never thought about that. I'm calling them now to give them a warning."

Richard appreciated the call. He told Lottie, "I would wait until we hear from the National Council before we hold any meetings or do any actions. Hopefully we will receive some word before next Sunday."

Abletown

Chapter 31 – Priscilla

Priscilla was meeting with Mr. Manor, the attorney for the trust. This was very difficult for her because she normally relied on friends to fight her battles for her. She would do anything possible to avoid confrontation. "Lately, I'm been spending so much time in the office at the senior center, that I wanted to asked about an offer you once made for me to use the third floor as an apartment."

Mr. Manor's eyebrows rose. "This is a bit of a surprise. You declined the offer once before, claiming it was important for you to have a separate space and to be with your friends. I can't think of a reason why you couldn't use the apartment but I do think we should have the Board vote on it."

FLAWED DECISIONS MURDER

Priscilla cringed. "Do you really think we need that? I'm the Trustee. I'm the one that makes the decisions."

Mr. Manor was paying total attention to the conversation. "What's going on Priscilla? Why this sudden decision?"

Priscilla didn't want to tell the truth. "I wouldn't say sudden. I've been thinking about it for a while. I was offered the use of the third floor, and it would be easier to use it and be there all the time. I don't like everyone knowing that the building is empty at night. What if someone wanted to vandalize the center? My being there might keep that from happening. I'm practically there all the time. It would just be easier for me to not have to make the trip home every day."

Mr. Manor chuckled, "In a town of 1,500, we don't really have a vandalizing problem. Your walk home is only three short blocks. Are you really going to tell me what is going on here?"

Priscilla didn't want to tell the truth so she used the secondary argument. "It would save me my social security check each month. I would be using some of the first month to put in a microwave and small refrigerator but after that, my expenses would be minimal. I quit doing water aerobics so there is no need to give the Friends Home that extra money.

136

MIA TENROC

Also, I would enjoy the privacy. No neighbors would mean no noise at night."

Mr. Manor looked concerned. "You were left a considerable sum of money by Mrs. Reid. Is there a problem with finances? You know I would be glad to help if I can." He could sense that Priscilla was still holding something back. Rather than badger her for more facts, he ended the meeting by saying, "Let me double check the rules of the trust and I will get back to you later today."

Immediately after Priscilla left, Mr. Manor called Jean. She was telling the morning story on the porch but took the call upon seeing who it was. "You are missing story time. Do you want to join us?"

Mr. Manor laughed, "Some of us keep business hours, otherwise I would be there. I heard your stories are really good. The reason I'm calling is that I had a strange visit from Priscilla today that has left me with questions. Upon the death of Mrs. Reid, Priscilla was offered the right to live on the third floor of the Reid house. Priscilla didn't want it at the time but now has requested the right to occupy it. I told her we needed a meeting of the Board of Directors for approval and she didn't want that to happen. Can you tell me what is going on here?"

Jean responded, "Eve, Belinda, Josephine and I are here. The only person missing is Fannie. We can

FLAWED DECISIONS MURDER

walk to her store and call you back if you want. Do you need all members or just a majority?" Mr. Manor confirmed the majority. Jean said, "Hold on a minute please." Jean put the phone on speaker. "Mr. Manor said Priscilla wants to move into the third floor of the Senior Center. He needs a majority vote to approve it. The offer to live there was made on the day Mrs. Reid died. What's your opinion?"

Josephine said, "It's ok with me. She obviously doesn't want to be here right now with us. I think a little distance would do her good."

Eve added, "I approve it too. Whatever make Priscilla happy is fine with me."

Belinda stated, "I agree that it would be best."

Jean said, "I'm sure Fannie wouldn't object either. I can have her call you if you like. You have my vote approving the residence based on one condition: only Priscilla alone can live there. No one else. If she has a visitor for a week, that would be understandable, but no one else can live there with her for more than a total of two weeks within a year."

Josephine agreed, "Good addition. My vote is based on it to be Priscilla alone. She has no right to give anyone else permission to live there without our approval."

MIA TENROC

Mr. Manor seemed relieved, "I know you aren't telling me the full story but I'm just glad to grant Priscilla's request and get this matter over with. Thank you."

Abletown

Chapter 32 – Identification

Janice turned to her partner, "Well, at least the identity of the victim was easy enough to determine. The license plate reads 'Trudy Must'. That is actually a humorous name for a prostitute. I can see that being a working name, but I still can't believe that's her actual name. It was like the poor judgment of her parents lead to her occupation. Anyways, it looks like she hasn't been picked up on prostitution charges recently."

Nick continued the thought. "Trudy is getting rather old for a woman in that profession. We need to find out if this murder was due to the hazard of the profession or if it was personal. You and I both assumed at the crime scene that she was killed by the hit on the back of her head. The corner confirmed

MIA TENROC

there was no water in the lungs. The shoe being wedged was another giveaway. I can't envision a shoe going into that position naturally. I guess today we will be pounding the pavement in her working neighborhood. Not a place we usually get honest answers from. The girls don't have a great love of the police."

They arrived at the pay-by-the-month hotel listed on the registration. "I have to protect the privacy of my customers. I don't answer questions without a warrant." The man behind the desk hardly looked up when reciting his answer.

Nick tried to reason, "The woman is dead. We have a warrant to search her room."

After reading the warrant, without saying a word, the dirty looking man grabbed some keys and lead the way. "I'm still not talking about my customers. You know what you are allowed to do and what you can't so go at it." He turned and walked away.

Nick said, "She has been murdered. Don't you care?"

The man paused and turned back. He actually had a look in his eye that showed sorrow. "She lived here for years. She was a good person in a bad life."

The initial look inside the room showed it wasn't a crime scene. The detectives started the long job of

FLAWED DECISIONS MURDER

looking through everything in the room for clues.
Trudy lived in this room for years and there were a lot
of material items accumulated. Every book would be
fanned through. Every CD covered opened and
reviewed. Without knowing why she was killed, the
difficulty was knowing what evidence they were
looking for. They bagged up many items like her
computer, paperwork, and checkbook.

This took them to mid-afternoon and signs of life
began happening in the neighboring units. They went
outside and decided to approach the separate units
alone. They would ask the person to talk in the
doorway or step outside. They didn't want to appear
threatening. Nick knocked on a door and a young
woman opened it. "Hi, I'm Detective Noble."

The woman immediately said, "If you don't have
a warrant, then beat it." Before he could respond, the
door was shut.

Janice was receiving the same treatment. At the
next door, she decided to start with, "Trudy is
deceased. She deserves justice. I am a detective and
want to see she gets a fair shake." The door wasn't
slammed shut immediately. "I'm not asking anything
about you. I just want to ask about Trudy. She died
last Saturday afternoon. Do you know if she was with
a customer?"

MIA TENROC

Seeing as how Janice's opening response worked, Nick started using it as well. When the door wasn't slammed shut, Nick would ask, "Could you come outside to talk? I don't want to appear inappropriate."

A couple of the ladies teased back, "Why not? You aren't bad looking."

Suddenly, Janice called him over to the person she was interviewing. The young lady said, "I know she wasn't working as long and hard as before, even though she was still active. She went away a lot in the afternoon, but I don't know if it was always the same customer. She seemed to be earning money but I don't know from where."

Janice instructed, "Please tell Detective Noble the other part, about the ladies that were here Monday."

The girl laughed, "Two ladies came here Monday afternoon showing Trudy's picture but kept calling her Missy. They certainly didn't belong in this neighborhood. They said she lost something at a place called Abletown. They said if she wanted it back, to go to the place Missy left on Friday afternoon at 2:00 p.m. I have no clue why Trudy would ever go to Abletown. That's a very strait-laced community. They were both maybe in their 50's or 60's. The one was not too descriptive. She was about my height, medium built, long dark hair, and very quiet. The other was blonde, very outgoing, about the same size as the

143

FLAWED DECISIONS MURDER

other lady, but the odd thing about her was that she had one blue eye and one green eye."

Janice thanked the girl very sincerely, while Nick stood with his mouth hanging open. In the car, Janice laughed, "Want to head to Abletown now or ask Jean and Fannie to come to the office?"

Nick answered with a groan.

Story

Chapter 33 – Plotting

Helena was confiding to her daughter, "I was surprised that Bob went with his original sermon. I knew he was having it recorded to upload for his final grade, but I had no idea he was streaming it live. He is out to destroy this church, to get me personally! I called to tell his online instructor that he was a failure, but before I could say anything, she told me how much she loved the sermon. I tried to explain that even though he came across okay on planned speeches, that in general he wasn't a likeable person. She seemed confused and said she would get back to me. I haven't heard anything for over 24 hours. I'm worried about what might be happening behind my back."

FLAWED DECISIONS MURDER

Grace suggested, "You have friends on the National Council. Why don't you call one of them to see if they know anything?"

Helena looked depressed, "Maybe she is just trying to decide for herself whether to believe me or interview him more. Your idea is a good one. I think I will wait another day, then I will call with some excuse to just chat with one of my friends. I'm sure that if something is going on, they will let me know. I don't want them to think there is a problem until I know there is."

Grace had another suggestion. "I'm sure they are plotting against you with our local board. After all, Lottie's the head of it and she has Bob living in her house, probably influencing her. We need to create a reason for Lottie to no longer trust Bob. She is extremely possessive, like she owns Bob. I've seen him talking to Violet a lot. They appear to be close friends. I'm sure Bob is the one that got Lottie, Richard, and maybe some others to vote Violet onto the Board. Richard was the one that said a spirit told him she should do it. We can start a gossip campaign or something."

Helena turned to the computer, "I'm looking up Lonnie's Facebook page. He lists where they are appearing so fans can find them. Bob is playing in Lonnie's band due to an injured member not being available. Lottie told me that Bob is uncomfortable with her going. He is claiming stage fright but we know that isn't true. I'm guessing there is a reason why he wants her to stay away. Look, they are playing at a local club Thursday through Sunday. Why don't we go over and check it out to see if there is a reason that he doesn't want Lottie to go?"

On Thursday night, Helena and Grace sat outside in their car watching the club door. They couldn't tell anything from that viewpoint so they snuck inside. The mother and daughter stood next to the wall at an angle where the band could not see them. After a brief moment, they turned and left. Grace asked, "Did you see Violet sitting at one of the tables? I think he might be seeing her on the side. I wonder if Lottie knows about this?"

Helena sounded devilish when she spoke, "Let's hope that's true. That would be just the right thing to create a wedge between the three of them. He already has Lottie if he really wanted her, so he must be after Violet. I understand her father is sick and she will inherit his business."

Grace pondered over her mother's comment. "Lottie already has money. If he was wanting a rich ride, why not go for the sure thing?"

FLAWED DECISIONS MURDER

Helena looked surprised, "Have you looked at Lottie's face? It's not good enough for a womanizer like Bob."

Grace laughed, "Violet looks better than Lottie but she's no raving beauty either. Let's play the card and see where it gets us."

Story

Chapter 34 – The Plan

Grace watched Lottie's home the following morning, knowing she would go to the grocery. She followed her at a distance. Lottie, lost in thought, didn't notice. As Lottie walked through the aisle, she looked up to see Grace headed her way with a few things in her cart. "Good morning, it's so good to see you, Lottie. Mom and I were talking this morning about wanting to get together with you."

Lottie was a little taken back, "Why would you want to see me? We are friends at church but it's not like we socialize after service."

Grace poured on the charm, "That's true but it's our mistake to correct. Are you available for dinner tonight? We would love to take you out. There is a new French restaurant we have been wanting to try on

FLAWED DECISIONS MURDER

Baker's Street. We would love it if you would be our guest."

The suspension was growing. Lottie wasn't sure she wanted to be alone with them. "I really don't think that is a good idea. I prepare dinner for Bob before he goes to work. I'm sure he is counting on me to be there."

Grace suggested, "Why don't you give him a call to see if he cares that you have some time on your own?"

Lottie made the call. "Bob, I have an offer for dinner tonight."

Before she could get another word out, he replied, "Good, you deserve a night off. I will grab a sandwich on the way to the club."

Lottie was kicking herself for not opening with the fact that the dinner was to be with Grace and Helena. She didn't believe he would approve of the dinner company. Since Grace heard Bob's response, she immediately said, "Wonderful! Why don't you meet Mom and I at the church about 6:00 this evening? We can drive."

Reluctantly, Lottie agreed. She decided it was best not to let Bob know because of his intense dislike of Helena and Grace. She thought maybe this was one of those meeting that was meant to be. Maybe she could talk to the ladies and get them to change their minds about Bob.

As soon as he hung up, Bob called Violet, "I was wondering if you would let me take you to dinner before the show tonight. Lottie has dinner plans, so I have the spare time. Besides, I've been wanting to ask you for some time."

Violet was blushing even though no one could see it. "Lottie will find out and not like it. I don't want her feelings hurt." Bob insisted it would be alright and plans were made.

At the restaurant that evening, Lottie was nervous. "I'm not sure why you wanted to take me to dinner. Considering the tension at church, I don't think this is the best idea."

Helena acted comforting. "I think that is even more reason for us to talk. Grace and I only want to do what is best for the church. We would welcome any ideas you have to make our services a happier and more inviting place to be."

Lottie really didn't know how to approach the subject of Bob. She started with, "Edgar suggested we have a lunch once a month. He offered to do the cooking and even pay for the food. Sometimes, when you break bread with someone, it can lead to nicer conversation."

FLAWED DECISIONS MURDER

Grace chimed in, "It certainly wouldn't hurt to give it a try."

Lottie continued a little timidly, "I think the festival we are planning will be a great connection to the neighborhood. Maybe we can also advertise monthly palm readings. We have enough people in the membership with that skill. We can use it as a method of advertising."

Helena said, "Agreed. That would be a possible draw. I think we should suggest it at the next council meeting."

Lottie tried to act brave, "Many members overheard the blow up between you and Bob last Sunday and it left a negative impression. I think an act of mending the fences would show compassion and maturity for both of you."

Helena wanted to get sick but instead said, "I do feel bad about the fight being overheard. I think extending the olive branch would be good. I'm willing to make the first step."

Grace turned the conversation to movies, music, and other topics not related to the church. The conversation flowed smoothly until the end of dinner. They exited the restaurant, which happened to be across the street from the club in which Bob was performing. Helena spontaneously suggested, "I want

152

MIA TENROC

to put the peace effort into effect immediately. Come with me ladies so you can witness my sincere efforts."

Lottie panicked. She knew Bob didn't want her going where he was performing, but she needed to be there to see what would occur. When they walked into the club, the band was on break. Bob was in the back alley talking with Violet. "I really want you to know that I am very fond of you. I appreciate you being here with me tonight. I'm grateful for your support at the church. I can see you making an excellent wife to some very lucky man. You emit such a soothing, calm feeling. Your friendship means so much. I hope I didn't embarrass you. I guess we better go back in. It's about time for me to go back on stage."

Violet didn't know what to say. She hoped Bob was thinking of her for the wife someday but he was still living with Lottie so she was confused. They walked in the door to see Lottie standing there next to the table she was using. "Lottie," she said, "It's so nice of you to come. This is my friend, Irene. She is married to Lonnie. I sit with her while her husband is on stage. Won't you please join us?"

Lottie initially felt anger and betrayal at seeing Violet and Bob together. She hoped Violet's explanation about her being in the club was true. Bob sensed Lottie looking at them and the door they just came through. He tried to cover the doubt, "I needed

FLAWED DECISIONS MURDER

some fresh air. Violet was nice enough to go out with me so I didn't have to stand alone. Also, that gives Lonnie time alone with his wife. I'm surprised you are here. Is everything ok?" It was then that Bob spotted Helena and Grace. "What are you two doing here?" His tone was seething. He then figured out this was a setup.

Helena came forward, "Lottie was telling me how bad it looked with our fight last week. I feel really bad about it. I don't want to go into any big discussion right now. I wanted to stop by and tell you that I hope you will come back to the church. You will be welcomed back."

Bob's ire was still escalating, "Lottie, you didn't tell me it was Helena and Grace that invited you to dinner. I don't think that was a wise idea."

Lottie was worried. She didn't want Bob to be angry. "You really didn't give me a chance to talk when I called you today. I'm so sorry you're upset. I thought maybe having a conversation over dinner would give me the opportunity to help end this war."

Bob turned to Helena. "Thank you for coming. I do intend to be at church on Sunday." His words were right but his voice still showed his displeasure and his eyes glared.

Lottie said to Violet, "Thanks for the invitation to join you. However, I need Helena to take me back to my car. I will see you at home, Bob."

Bob spoke softly enough for only Lottie to hear. "Maybe."

Helena and Grace felt they had their victory. Lottie still was upset over Violet but didn't know how to take the surprise meeting. Bob knew this was a setup to put Lottie and Violet at odds. Violet knew that Bob was using Lottie and began to wonder if he was just using her too.

Abletown

Chapter 35 – Jean's Questioning

Tempers escalated a little in the car when Janice suggested, "Do you want me to interview Jean and you interview Fannie about their asking questions on the deceased?"

Nick responded, "Jean is my wife. We exchanged vows in the church even though we didn't file the marriage certificate. She would never lie to me if I asked her a direct question. Why wouldn't I interview my own wife?"

Janice realized she didn't choose her words correctly. "I didn't say that Jean would lie to you. I just thought I would make the offer. Would you prefer that I interview Fannie?"

MIA TENROC

Nick glanced over at this partner. They had been together for over ten years now. He knew she didn't mean to offend him. "I think we should talk to Jean and then decide if we need to interview Fannie. I'm sure Jean is the one investigating. She uses Fannie to get people to talk more freely. Why don't we call her now?" The phone rang and Jean answered. Nick spoke, "Hello, my love. Before we begin, you are on speaker and Janice is in the car."

"Hi Jean," Janice said.

Jean laughed, "Hi. Good thing you told me so I wouldn't say something inappropriate."

Nick continued, "If you aren't busy, I was hoping you could come up for tonight. I have a couple of things I wanted to ask you about, and if you're driving up, you might as well spend the night. I'm in the mood for a romantic evening."

Jean replied with a sexy voice, "Boy, that is too tempting to pass up. What time and where do you want to meet?"

Nick answered, "I was wondering if you could meet us at the police station?"

Jean replied, "Whoa, you told me never to go to the station. You said you would get in trouble if the Captain saw me there."

FLAWED DECISIONS MURDER

Nick replied, "I know, that's true. To be honest, before our evening together, I wanted you to look at a dead body. I wondered if you knew who she was?"

Jean responded sourly, "This isn't sounding too romantic. I bet Janice even wants to be there."

It was Janice's turn to laugh out loud. "I only want to be there to see if you know the victim. I promise not to go to Nick's place with you."

Jean started to ask questions, but Nick cut off the conversation. "We are going into the office now. Please, just hurry over to the station and we can over the details then."

It was a twenty-minute drive for Jean. With taking a few minutes to pack a suitcase and letting the front desk of the Friend's Home know she wouldn't be there for dinner or breakfast, it took Jean about 40 minutes to arrive. Jean paused by Priscilla's door before leaving. Normally Jean would tell Priscilla that she was departing but since the dispute about the mayor's race, Priscilla quit talking to Jean in the evenings. She didn't attend the porch time stories or water aerobics, so Jean decided she wouldn't bother with the consideration she would normally have shown. Nick greeted her with a hug when she arrived. Right then, the Captain walked out of the office. "What are you doing here?"

MIA TENROC

Jean smiled, "Really? Not a 'Hello, how are you, Jean?' You could have said, 'Good to see you, Jean.' You really need to work on your social skills."

The Captain looked at Nick, "Is she involved in another one of your cases?"

Nick said calmly, "I don't think 'involved' is the right word. Jean saw a naked lady in the woods the other day. I wondered if it was the same woman as our victim. We are about to go view the body."

The Captain turned to Jean, "Do you often see naked ladies in the woods?"

Jean smiled, "Not if I can help it. I'm too modest for that."

The Captain turned to Janice and Nick. "Keep me informed about what is going on." To Jean, he said, "Murder just seems to follow you." He turned and walked away.

Jean didn't say any more in the office but walked quietly to the morgue. Seeing a dead body didn't bother Jean. Being a reporter on the crime beat, Jean saw her share of sordid things. The drawer was pulled out and the cover removed. She looked at the corpse and then left. Outside, she said, "That woman was working in Leon Pierre's campaign office. Belinda is totally backing Leon for Mayor because he opposes big developers coming in to tear down the stately old

FLAWED DECISIONS MURDER

homes in Abletown. Belinda works in his office in the afternoons. She told me about a woman named Missy that was throwing herself at Leon. It disgusted her. Many men are fools to think a younger woman is attracted to them for who they are. I figured it was because she wanted something, even though scoring a small-town mayor isn't exactly hitting the big time. I followed her after work last Friday afternoon. She didn't even know she was being tailed. It's not like I'm really that good at it. I thought I would follow her up the highway one day. The next time I would be at that exit to follow her a little further. I just stayed with her since she never seemed to notice me. I followed her to a cheap hotel that houses many ladies of the evening. When I saw where she was staying, I left."

Nick asked, "Is she the same woman that you saw naked in the woods on Saturday?"

Jean nodded yes. "I wasn't totally honest with you that day. I knew Leon had a hunting cabin in the woods. I saw Missy standing in the backyard in a robe. I saw Leon pull up and get out. He walked over to Missy and said something to her. I couldn't tell what was said, only that Leon was clearly unhappy. Missy dropped her robe and tried to kiss Leon but he just pushed her away, walked to his car and left. Missy fell to the ground but was in a sitting position. I don't believe she was hurt."

160

MIA TENROC

Janice's jaw dropped in surprise about what she just heard. Nick's expression became serious as he pressed for more information. "What happened next?"

Jean stated in a matter-of-fact tone, "The viewfinder went dead. The time ran out. I hurried to get another quarter out of my purse, but I dropped the coin and you were yelling for me to hurry. I finally found the quarter and inserted it in the slot but by then, Leon was gone. There was a truck up the road a little way from the house on the other side of the street. It looked like a green truck, maybe a Ford Ranger. You know a mid-size. I saw a man in the woods nearby but I didn't see him there when all this took place between Missy and Leon."

Janice asked, "Did you know him? Can you give a description?"

Jean responded, "No. Sorry. I only saw him from the back. He wasn't near a house or anything to judge his height. He was white. I would guess he was middle age because of the width of his butt." Janice laughed but Jean ignored her. "Men do spread with time, you know. He had on medium blue jeans, a dark blue jacket like an older man would wear. There was a leather strap around his back and over his shoulder. It wasn't a backpack so I would guess a camera strap or that of a pair of binoculars. His hair was brown but he had on a ball cap so I can't tell you if it was long or

161

FLAWED DECISIONS MURDER

short because it may have been tucked under the hat. He had an odd birthmark on his neck, like a semi-circle on the bottom with a couple of jet ups on the top."

Nick said aloud, "He might not have anything to do with this murder. It could be a nature lover, but it's hard to say. Any more information?"

Jean replied, "No, or I would have said it. I can draw a picture of his neck, if you like."

Abletown

Chapter 36 – Dinner

Nick kept his promise and took Jean out for what would have been a romantic dinner if Janice wasn't tagging along. When they were heading to their table, they were surprised to see Connor and Eve dining together. The couple didn't see them so Nick, Jean and Janice continued to their table which was out of sight of the one the two were sitting at. Janice asked, "What is going on there?"

Jean replied, "They profess to being friends. I'm not sure where this is going since Eve is so much older than Connor. I guess the important thing is that they enjoy each other's company. I think both need a good friend right now in their life. Let's stay on task. I know you have more questions. Why don't we get them out of the way so Nick and I can concentrate on

FLAWED DECISIONS MURDER

ourselves instead when we get home? Also, does Janice have to stay with us all night? No offense, Janice."

Nick admitted Jean was right. "We know you and Fannie went to the hotel where this woman you call Missy lived to ask some questions."

"Oh?" Jean's eyes widened. "You must have talked to the one little girl that would answer any questions. The desk clerk and the other residents wouldn't speak to us. Was she in room 36?"

Janice laughed, "You really should have been a detective. We are waiting to hear about the hotel and also more on the Mayor's race."

Jean, knowing it was the only way to get Nick alone, obliged, "I took Fannie to the hotel with me because I felt unsafe going alone." Nick made a good girl comment which Jean ignored. "Fannie can get a dead person to talk, whereas people usually ignore me. I told her about all that was happening and stood back while she worked her magic. The girl at the hotel said that Missy was getting a little old for most customers, but some older men don't want to feel like they are doing something nasty to their child and appreciate a more mature woman. She also said that Missy wasn't working the streets as much at night. She did have a flow of money coming in. Missy hadn't said anything about Abletown or Leon. I got so

164

MIA TENROC

mad when the girl assumed that Fannie and I might be interested in a relationship. She said Missy didn't do women."

Nick and Janice laughed for longer than Jean thought was necessary. Jean gave them a dirty look before continuing, "We really didn't find out anything from our trip except that Missy was a woman for hire. Regarding the Mayor's race, Peter has been Mayor for at least 20 years. A town of 1500 isn't going to pay much but Peter never had much ambition. He wants to buy a house in the woods, his wife wants to stay in town. His wife also said that they don't have much saved towards retirement. There are housing developers what want to come in and tear down our historic houses. Abletown is famous for antiques. No one wants to go to a modern city to shop and the new housing would destroy our only source of business. There is also a problem with the additional cost of utilities that would need to be upgraded, additional teachers, and losing our small-town feel. Most of our residents realize that development will happen but we want the downtown district to be protected with a historic zoning ordinance. There are plenty of farms that are going under that are willing to sell out so we feel the developers can build there. We want there to be fees added to each housing project to cover the additional costs the town will incur, be it utilities or

FLAWED DECISIONS MURDER

improvement in roads. I believe Peter is willing to sell out the town and pocket the money for himself."

Nick thought, "I think all that you said about the town improvement makes good sense. Aren't the residents all in agreement on those matters?"

Jean looked sad, "There are some people that only view Peter as a good man. They don't believe he would sell the town out. The majority see it like I do. The town is becoming very split. Leon believes Peter will not do right for the town. Leon retired from being the Mayor of another town. He doesn't really want to go back into politics but Leon invested a lot of money in his new home in Abletown. He doesn't want his house to lose its value, that is why Leon is running. He and Peter are, or rather, were actually friends, which is why the town is becoming more divided on this campaign. It's like choosing one friend over the other."

Nick said, "I guess I should spend more time in Abletown. I didn't realize things were getting so heated."

Jean nodded, "I guess you should hang out at Fannie's or the diner to get all the local new. I know you don't like gossip but I think that might be a way to find out about the murder."

MIA TENROC

Janice looked surprised, "Do you think either Leon or Peter murdered Missy, or I should say Trudy, which is her real name."

Jean replied, "I don't know. Missy was still working, so it might have been a customer gone bad. I just don't understand why a big city working girl would work on Leon's campaign and make passes at him. Ok, I have another confession of something I haven't told you yet. I have a spy in Peter's headquarters." Both detectives were leaning forward, eager for the news. "I want to know the truth before I vote. I asked Eve to work at Peter's headquarters because she is friends with him. She is his bookkeeper on his private business and does his taxes. I figure if there is anyone he trusts, it's Eve. She feels guilty but she also wants to know the truth. Peter is paying a photographer more than he should. Peter is also paying an outside consultant that no one has even met. He is making the checks payable to cash so we don't know their names. I would start there."

Nick pushed further, "I know you told me all the facts. Now, tell me your hunch."

Jean stated, "I would guess that Peter is paying Missy to make a pass at Leon so he would be discredited. Our small town holds people to high moral values. I think the photographer was hired to catch the evidence so Peter can smear Leon's

167

FLAWED DECISIONS MURDER

reputation. I really believe it after Missy's naked show on Saturday."

Janice said, "I think you might be right. Missy died shortly after the altercation with Leon. I guess we will start work in Abletown tomorrow morning. I got the hint, now that everything is out, I will make myself scarce so you two can enjoy your evening alone.

Story

Chapter 37 – New Allies

Violet called Lottie the next morning after the tense encounter, "Are you alone? Can you talk?"

Lottie had debated whether to accept the call when she saw it was Violet. Lottie was hurt, angry, and unsure of her next step. Realizing that she would have to face Violet at church eventually, she decided to accept the call. "I'm doing some shopping, so yes, I can talk without anyone overhearing me."

Violet asked, "Are you ok? I was worried about you since you appeared to be distraught last night."

Lottie blushed, "I hope I didn't make a fool of myself. I felt stupid. Bob never wanted me to go watch him play, now I know it's because he was meeting you."

FLAWED DECISIONS MURDER

Violet wanted to make things clear. "I told Bob that my father has been given only a few months to live. I'm so depressed. I really don't have many friends in this town. I believe he invited me as a distraction from my sadness and depression. He did pay for dinner last night, which was the first time we ever went to eat. We had a serious talk about my situation, and he offered to be there to help me. Other than that, I pay for my own drinks. We are not dating. I have gotten to be friends with the wives of the other band members. I appreciate the escape from my thoughts but I assure you that there is nothing going on between Bob and myself."

Lottie was sincere when she exclaimed, "I'm so sorry! I didn't know what you are going through on a personal basis. Thank you for explaining. I mean it when I say if there is anything I can do, please let me know. You shouldn't have to feel alone. You should be able to rely on your church family."

Violet let out a snort, "Right, like how your church family was supporting you when they were leading you into an embarrassing situation last night. I don't trust Helena or Grace at all. I noticed that when someone confides in them, that information ends up being used against them in the future. I believe Lisette has a good heart. She would be a church member that I would trust, except that she doesn't understand how evil Helena is. While the rest of us know to distrust

MIA TENROC

Grace around money, Lisette chooses to believe Grace's profession of innocence. Most of all, she hasn't realized yet that Bob has a crush on her."

That last sentence was a slap on the face to Lottie. It confirmed the truth about her chances with Bob. "Let's meet up for lunch. I would appreciate talking to you. It might be beneficial for both of us to be on the same page about Bob and our position on things at the church." Violet agreed and they made arrangements to meet in an hour at a restaurant with a quiet dining area.

At the luncheon, Lottie expressed her new-found revelations. "You made me realize that it was me pursuing Bob. He is good-looking and can be charming when he wants to be. There is really nothing going on between us. We don't hug, kiss, date, or anything that would move towards the relationship I hoped would happen. He has done a great job on fixing up my house. I recommended him for the janitor job at church, and he did a good job there as well. He has never given me any false hopes that he could be interested in me."

Violet could hear the shaking in Lottie's voice. She could sense that Lottie was very hurt. "You are a good person, Lottie. I don't believe Bob understands what a good friend you are, and that his life would be better with you in it."

FLAWED DECISIONS MURDER

Lottie looked up, "I can look in the mirror and see I don't have a face that would attract a man. I had always hoped that my good heart would appeal to someone."

Violet gave a kind of chuckle, "You are talking to someone that is built too low to the ground. Being so short, everything I eat ends up lying on my hips. Men don't like women that are on the stocky side."

Lottie's hands went on her hips. "Violet, you are a wonderful person. You have a sense of peace that makes people enjoy your company. You have a pretty face. Don't harbor such negative things about yourself."

Violet smiled, "See what I mean when I say you are a good person? I think us meeting together to get things in the right perspective was a good idea. While Bob has shown me nothing but friendship, I got a strange feeling that I shouldn't trust him. He says that he wants to be there for me and with me when I go through the ordeal with my father. I'm not sure if that is because of friendship, or because he knows I will inherit the family business. I think he wants to take over running one of our stores."

Lottie gave this some thought. "While I did say that he did a good job for me at home and at the church, I don't know that I trust him either. I think he is using me, but I did extend that opportunity to him. I would test his bedroom door at night but he always kept it locked. After the event at the club, he knew that he lost me as his supporting friend. Last night, the roles were reversed, where he tried my bedroom door and found it to be locked. He never wanted me before so this means I don't trust him. I think he will do whatever is necessary to get his way. I really feel a need to ask him to leave. Please tell me your opinion on what I should do."

Violet replied, "Now that you know that there is no hope of a relationship with Bob, if you don't feel like you can continue being friends, then I would ask him to leave." Lottie appreciated Violet's honesty. Violet then changed the subject. "Somehow Helena found out that I go to the club to listen to the band. I also believe she deliberately took you there in order to divide us. She wants Bob out of the church so badly, she would stop at nothing to get her way."

Lottie added clarity to that issue. "Bob wants to be a Pastor because he sees Helena as a con-woman that makes money easily without working. I think he feels our religion is fake but he doesn't care as long as he can make money at it. Bob wants to get rid of Helena because she stands in his way of getting the Pastor license. I think that is why he wants Lisette to become the Head Pastor, because she would sign off on him receiving his license. Personally, I want Helena gone simply because I don't like nor trust her.

FLAWED DECISIONS MURDER

I guess on this issue Bob and I agree that Helena should be voted out of the church."

Violet wanted to confirm some facts. "I also think it would be best for the church if Helena were gone. If I recall, Helena's sister previously owned the building and was the Pastor until she died. Did Helena inherit the title to it?"

Lottie knew the answer, "Helena's sister, Donna, specifically left the building to the church organization. Thus, we are able to vote Helena out and keep the building. I knew Donna and she was a really good person. Everyone loved her. I'm so glad we talked today. I feel so much better."

Violet smiled, "I feel better, too. I think we are on the same page about the church, Helena, Grace and Bob. What are you going to say when you get home? Are you going to tell Bob we had lunch together?"

"Absolutely," said Lottie. "I probably won't say anything else. I will text and let you know what happens."

Story

Chapter 38 – More Truth

When Lottie returned home, she put on a happy face and smiled as she greeted Bob. "Good afternoon. I did the grocery shopping today. I picked up those cookies you like so well. Are you going to be here for dinner?"

Bob was surprised. He thought Lottie would be angry. "Do you want to talk about last night?"

Lottie acted surprised, "If you have something you want to say, we can. If not, I'm good. Violet and I had lunch today. We are on the same page about everything." Bob wondered what that meant but was afraid to pursue it. Lottie continued, "I just wish you would have told me about her father. We both need to be there to support her through this difficult time. She and I plan to spend more time together doing fun

FLAWED DECISIONS MURDER

things." Bob was speechless. Lottie ignored him, "I think it is wonderful that you are there for her. She has enjoyed going to your performances at the club. I do hope you will invite her again."

Bob could hardly speak, "I didn't think you would understand. I thought you would have been upset over my spending time with Violet."

Lottie ignored his comment and asked, "Did you ever answer if you would be here for dinner? If you are here, I will make a pork roast. If you aren't, I will enjoy a salad."

Bob said, "I will be here. I hate to make you do extra work for me. I would enjoy the roast but a salad would be fine. I think I will go out and work in the yard this afternoon. It is a beautiful day. I will be glad to work on any other tasks you have on your honey-do-list."

Lottie cheerfully answered, "No, I think making the yard look better would be nice." She walked off to her bedroom and closed the door. She kept up the fake happiness as long as she could. The reality check had been hard on Lottie. She took a couple of pills for a headache and laid down for a nap."

She got back up and was cooking dinner when Bob came in from outside. "It must really be hot out there. You look very drained."

176

MIA TENROC

Bob smiled, "I smell bad, too. I will keep my distance. I'm heading for the shower. I admit I didn't sleep good last night. I'm so glad we are ok."

Lottie thought he was actually sincere. She continued working in the kitchen when she heard a phone ring. Bob had left his phone on the table. Lottie went over and looked at the incoming call. There was a picture of a young man and the name Zack showed on the screen. She didn't know what to do. What if it was an emergency? She slid the bar over to answer. "Zack, you don't know me. I'm your father's roommate, nothing more. Bob is in the shower right now. I was afraid it would be an emergency and wanted to let you know to hold on and I will get Bob out of the shower right now."

Zack answered, "It's not an emergency. I haven't spoken to my father since I left. I'm hurt that he hasn't even tried to call me. I wanted him to know that I don't hate him for what he did. He was a good father in some ways. I'm happy living with my mother and don't want to come home. I just wanted to let him know."

Lottie was shocked, "I'm sorry, Zack. I don't know exactly what happened when you left. I somehow got the feeling you had an illness and that's why you live with your mother."

FLAWED DECISIONS MURDER

Zack started to get angry, "No, I'm perfectly healthy. I left because Bob told me my mother was dead. When I found her, I wanted to meet her and be with her. That's why I left. Is Bob lying again? I regret calling. Please delete this call from the phone if you can and don't tell him I called. If he ever did care for me, he would try to mend the fence. In case you don't know it, his cell phone password is 9564. Will you do that for me, Lottie?"

Lottie was stunned. "I certainly will. I wish you the best, Zack. Do you want my number, in case you ever want to reach me?"

Zack said no and hung up. Lottie keyed in Bob's password into his phone and deleted the call from the incoming call list. She placed the phone in the exact spot where Bob had left it. She was trying to put the finishing touches on the dinner while her mind was spinning with the information she had just learned. All that Bob told the church and the members about his son having an illness and was dying was a lie. Bob walked into the room and spoke. Lottie jumped and let out a squeak. "What's wrong with you?" asked Bob.

Lottie laughed, "I was deep in thought. I didn't hear you coming into the room. I'm just about to put dinner on the table."

MIA TENROC

Bob walked over, glanced at his phone, and put it into his pocket. He walked over and gave Lottie a hug. "You are such a good friend. My life is so much better having you in it."

Lottie thought to herself, you sure are better off. Her skin felt repulsed at his touch. This man made up a lie, using his son in a horrible way, just to get people to feel sorry for him. All Lottie wanted was for Bob to leave her alone. She needed time to think. She didn't know if she should tell anyone. Just then, she remembered that she had told Violet earlier that she would be there for her. Lottie wondered if she should warn Violet about how much of a liar Bob really was.

Abletown

Chapter 39 – Investigation Starts

"A betrayal of friendship is what I think Jean and Priscilla are both feeling. Belinda and Jean said quite a bit before finding out Priscilla's loyalty to Peter. From the way Jean tells it, there are anywhere from fifty to one hundred million dollars involved. Most people want the main part of downtown protected, even though they realize growth will happen. Belinda has gone to all the property owners in the downtown area and explained why they should vote for Leon. Jean and Josephine are researching homes to see if they qualify for the National Historic Register. If they do, they are going to the property owners and explaining the pros and cons of listing their house. If the owners want their house to be listed as historic, Jean and Josephine are helping with the paperwork.

MIA TENROC

They figure if enough houses are listed, it will keep the developers out." This was Nick's answer to Janice when she asked if a little town like Abletown could actually be the reason for the murder. "Jean begged me to let her work with us. She knows how the boss feels but when she is on the scent, she is a blood hound. Jean isn't saying much but it appears she is troubled because Priscilla doesn't associate with the other friends any longer and has moved into the Reid house."

Janice was very surprised. "Priscilla would likely be sitting in jail right now when she was falsely accused of murder a couple years ago if it wasn't for Jean's investigative effort. Jean certainly proved herself to be a good friend to Priscilla. Obviously, Priscilla doesn't appreciate the friendship enough to let a simple mayoral race come between her and her companions."

Nick didn't reply but reached for the ringing phone. "They are ready for us at the coroner's office. Let's make a plan of attack after we hear the report. I did ask for some help from Detective Maloney from Vice. I got a voicemail from her. She said that Trudy didn't walk the streets. It appears she had some regulars. She also suggests we talk to Sister Mary at the Mission. It is an outreach that tries to get girls off the street and into a regular job and life."

FLAWED DECISIONS MURDER

The coroner greeted them when they arrived. "I don't have everything complete yet but I wanted you to know that Trudy was dead before she went into the water. Her neck was broken, and there are wood fibers indicating that she either fell or was struck by a piece of raw wood. There is no evidence of any kind of finish or varnish on it. Most likely it was a stump of a tree that she fell back on due to the upward angle. If someone was striking her with a piece of wood it would be more of a 90-degree angle. I'm sure the time of death was about an hour before she was in the water. The watch stopped because of the water, not the time of death."

The detectives thanked him and went out to talk. Nick suggested, "Let's start at the Mission. What else did you find on the checkbook and calendar you were going through this morning?"

Janice answered, "She used initials instead of names. There appears to be about 10 different customers. Some were weekly, while others were once a month or so. From the other angle, I saw the entries in the checking account that correspond with the dates and times Jean told us about. I got a warrant to get the records from the bank."

At the Mission, Sister Mary was greatly saddened by the news. "Trudy actually liked her work, and while she would come visit me, she never gave any

MIA TENROC

indication of changing her lifestyle. She didn't relate to the young girls on the street, and there aren't many her age where she lives, so she would come to talk to me. She has been asking if her new style of dress looked more respectable. She wanted to come across as high-class. She indicated that she was after a big mark, a very respectable man. She said if things worked out right, she would come into a nice nest egg. I'm not sure who or what she was doing for this payday but she did have high hopes."

The detectives thanked Sister Mary and left for their next stop at the bank that Trudy used. The customer service representative produced pictures of the deposits. "These are copies of money orders. All were purchased at the 1st National Bank at the Abletown office."

Armed with the copies of the money orders, Nick and Janice headed to the bank in Abletown. Janice asked, "Do we need to get another warrant?"

Nick replied, "Probably not. I've been to a picnic a couple of times with the branch manager and I think he will be cooperative."

Sam Smith saw them when they entered the branch and came out to greet Nick. "So good to see you. Are you here just for banking or is there something I can help you with?"

183

FLAWED DECISIONS MURDER

Nick suggested going to Sam's office and closed the door. "Sam, this is my partner, Janice Hoover. We are here on official business." Nick produced a picture of Trudy. "Have you ever seen this woman before?" Sam studied the picture and shook his head no before handing it back. Nick continued, "She was murdered on Saturday the 4th of this month. It is my understanding she was in Abletown in the afternoon for a few weeks or more. These money orders have been deposited into her checking account and they were obtained from this office."

Sam examined the money orders, noticing the date and amounts. "I'm going to take these out and ask our tellers if they know who purchased them." Sam left the office and went behind the teller counter and talked to two ladies there. There were no customers in the bank right then so the conversation happened quickly without interruption. Sam returned, "The tellers said that they were purchased by Peter using checks from the re-election campaign. They said there are other money orders that he purchased. They gave me those number."

Janice looked curious, "How would they know that without even consulting the paperwork?"

Sam laughed, "You must have never lived in a small town. There isn't much action here. Money order purchases are uncommon. For Peter to purchase

184

MIA TENROC

the money orders using campaign money, he has created a fair amount of gossip with the employees here. Peter is a nice enough guy but I don't consider him very smart in some ways. The purchases could be a campaign violation."

Nick stood and shook hands with Sam. "You've been a big help. I thank you for the information. Please don't tell anything about the picture I showed you and the murder. I would like to talk to Peter without any warning."

Sam laughed again. "Do you see how those employees are looking in here? They will attack me for information the minute you walk out the door. I won't tell them anything but they will hound me for the rest of the day. They will probably go home mad when I don't answer their questions."

Nick smiled, "You can blame me for the silence."

Abletown

Chapter 40 – Town Gossip

When Jean arrived home that morning, it was much earlier than when she usually got up. She was already sitting on the porch with her first cup of green tea when Josephine, Eve and Belinda arrived. Josephine commented, "Something is up. There is no way you would be so wide awake and dressed that nice just to see us."

Jean blushed, "Nick invited me out to dinner last night. I spent the night and just got back about 15 minutes ago."

Belinda asked, "Are you going to tell us why you went up in the middle of the week? Is there a mystery going on?"

MIA TENROC

Trying to avoid the conversation being about her, she turned to Eve. "Did you enjoy your dinner last night?"

Eve looked surprised. "How did you know I went out to dinner? Are you spying on me?"

Jean smiled, "We happened to eat at the same place last night. Nick and I wanted to talk alone so we didn't come over to say anything."

Belinda turned to Eve, "Who did you go out with?"

Eve replied, "Connor is just a friend. Nick and Jean introduced us. My husband, Nigel, won't take me out. He stays at the farm all the time. Connor is too young for me. He is going through a divorce and is feeling a little low. We talk and laugh about a wide range of topics. It helps him relief stress. He trusts me and uses me not only as a distraction, but also as someone to confide in. There is nothing going on."

Belinda looked at Josephine and nodded, "We think you are protesting too much."

Jean returned to telling her story for about an hour before the ladies headed to Fannie's place for their afternoon tea. Fannie greeted them with, "Jean, why is Nick in town? He and Janice just came out of the bank. They then headed to Peter's headquarters. What is going on?"

FLAWED DECISIONS MURDER

Jean just looked at her and said nothing. Josephine fussed at her sister, "How can you not tell us if there is a mystery happening?"

Jean answered, "It is an open case that Nick is working on. I'm not permitted to discuss it until he says I can. Not only could I mess up the investigation, but I might accidentally tip off the bad guys."

Fannie shouted, "Who is the bad guy?"

Jean replied, "I don't know for sure. If I did then Nick wouldn't need to investigate."

Fannie pulled out the newspaper and was looking at the stories. She also turned on the local news program. "When the story comes up, I should be able to tell by Jean's reaction which one Nick is working on. After all, Jean doesn't have a poker face." It wasn't long before the story about a car being pulled from the lake with a dead body in it aired on the television. Fannie turned, "That was it! I can tell. Who was the person?"

The picture of the victim appeared on the screen. Belinda jumped up. "That's Missy! She is the one that was working on Leon's campaign that I didn't like. She doesn't belong in this town and the way she flirted with him was really ridiculous. Am I right, Jean? Was Missy the victim?"

188

MIA TENROC

Jean reluctantly responded, "Yes. I saw the body last night and identified her. I told Nick about her volunteering to work for Leon. I told him what we all know. I guess it doesn't hurt since you already figured it out."

Belinda asked, "Did you tell them about Missy making a pass at Leon?"

Jean nodded yes. "We really shouldn't say anything to anyone else. Let the town gossip but don't confirm or comment on anything. We are getting to the murder portion of our story. That will give another thing for our brains to work on."

Story

Chapter 41 – Action

Lottie woke up Sunday morning feeling empowered. Today the committee will vote on the offices in the church. After the underhanded way Helena and Grace tricked her, she wanted them out. She wondered if she should tell the truth to anyone about Bob's lie. Violet and her friendship had started less than 24 hours before. Violet knew how much she wanted Bob and chose to meet him on the sly. Lottie figured that Violet would be her best chance of getting Bob out of her home without him realizing how much she wanted him to leave. She decided to not tell Violet for now. There was one person she did plan to tell, depending on the outcome of the elections today.

MIA TENROC

Bob was eating some breakfast when she walked into the kitchen. "Good morning, Bob. The big vote to get rid of Helena is today. I made lunch for the committee. After the service, we will dine and then have the business meeting. Sorry if that messes up your cleaning schedule."

Bob was smiling. "I don't mind working later tonight at all. It is so worth the change of schedule, hoping for a change in the church. You seem rather chipper today."

Lottie picked up the box and was headed out the door when she said, "I feel today will be really important. See you there."

Bob cleaned up the dishes and reached for his phone and keys. He checked his phone to see if Violet had called. They usually talked a few times a day, but she hadn't called last night. When the phone lit up, Bob noticed something was wrong. He always left his phone with all windows shut down, but this time the screen immediately displayed the phone function. He looked for recent calls and found nothing new. "I wonder if Lottie is searching my phone? If so, why would she be happy about seeing all those calls with Violet?"

With Lottie out of the house, Bob used her computer to spy on his son. Since Zack was still on his cell phone bill, he looked at the list of recent calls

191

FLAWED DECISIONS MURDER

and noticed that his son phoned him last night. He then attempted to contact his son, but it was his ex-wife that answered. "I want to talk to Zack."

Judy replied, "He handed me his phone because he doesn't want to talk to you."

Bob shouted, "You're lying! He called me last night. I want to talk to him, now!"

Zack's voice came on the phone. "What do you want?"

Bob spoke in a very kind voice, "I miss you, son. I saw on the phone list that you called me yesterday. I'm so glad. I thought you wouldn't speak to me, which is why I didn't bother to contact you before now. Did you want something?"

Zack was very upset. "Lottie promised me she would delete the call. Is she as much of a liar as you are?"

Bob tried to stay in control. "She did as you requested and didn't tell me about it. I was looking online at recent calls and saw the entry. Why did you ask her to delete the call?"

Zack explained, "Lottie saw that it was me calling by the picture on the screen. She answered very worried, thinking that it was an emergency, and even offered to get you out of the shower. She then asked how I was feeling and if I was still in the

MIA TENROC

hospital. That's when I found out that you were telling people that I was dying in order to get sympathy. I don't know what con you are pulling this time, but I will not be your tool. Although I would never leave my mother again, I called hoping that we could still have some sort of a relationship. But when I heard what Lottie said, I gave up on that idea and just asked her to delete the call and not tell you."

Bob tried to justify his actions, "Son, I had to explain your absence and didn't want to confess what I did to your mother. I told a lie and it just grew. I didn't say anything bad about you. I'm active in a church and wanted them to pray for you. I was hoping that those prayer would lead to your return."

Zack became even more disgusted, "I'm getting a new phone number under my mom's plan so you can't track my calls, since I now know that's what you've been doing. You might as well cancel this number. I won't use it again. If I can ever forgive this new lie, I might call you, but for now, don't bother contacting me again." The line went dead. Bob tried to redial but there was no answer. It went straight to voicemail.

Bob tried to think as he drove to church, "I don't understand why Lottie is so happy. I would think she would have been miserable knowing that I had lied." When Bob arrived, the service was well on its way.

FLAWED DECISIONS MURDER

Violet and Lottie were sitting together. There was an older man sitting next to Violet that had to be her father. Bob started to worry and considered leaving but then Violet spotted him and motioned him over. She scooted over so he could sit between her and Lottie.

Violet whispered, "This is my father. He came without telling me ahead of time. I will explain things later." There was no more conversation until the service ended. Violet stood up and made introductions. "My father has non-tribal members call him Grey. I have a favor to ask you, Bob. This vote today is very important. Why don't you take my father to lunch and get to know each other? I will call you when the meeting is over. Is that ok for you, Father?"

The two men left. The ladies chatted over lunch. Helena and Grace were staring. Their plan to divide and conquer hadn't work. There was no way for them to know what was to occur.

Story

Chapter 42 – The Showdown

Lottie called the meeting to order. "We need nominations for the position of Head Pastor."

One person said, "Helena, of course. She's always been the leader of this church." Another person nominated Lisette, which surprised her. There were no other nominations. The vote was taken. It was 8 to 4 in favor of Lisette. Helena sat in silence but her anger showed.

The next position voted on was the secretary/bookkeeper. The person that nominated Helena said she wanted Grace. Another person added Paul Myers to the list and a third member suggested Cindy Cotte. The vote was completed with Paul Myers winning the position.

FLAWED DECISIONS MURDER

Helena jumped up from her chair and yelled at the board. "How dare you vote against my daughter and I! We, along with my sister, created this church! It is ours and you can't take it away from us! You will be hearing from our attorney! Even if we leave, you will be paying dearly to use our church!"

A woman on the board who happened to be an attorney stood, "Your sister left this property to the church. There is nothing in the will or the by-laws that states it is dependent on your being Pastor. There is nothing that says you personally have any rights. The honest truth is you abuse your position. You gossip about things told in confidence. You try to control and manipulate people instead of serving them. We are just tired of your demeaning ways."

The woman that ran the festival spoke next. "I had each booth and tent keep records of exactly how much profit was made to determine the food and activities for next year. There is $500.00 missing that I know we raised and was not deposited. You made all these excuses when we had the accountant review our books. You claimed everything was balanced in the end, even if things were posted incorrectly. A few of us started putting marked money in the collection plate as a test, so we know Grace took it out and didn't report it. The missing $500.00 is the last straw. She is to never touch the church funds again."

MIA TENROC

The four board members that were in favor of Helena started shouting. "You are making too big a deal over nothing." "It was their church so it really is their money." "If they leave the church, then we will go with them."

Lottie stood up and called order to the meeting. "I think it is up to Helena and Grace if they wish to leave the church, and if any of you go, that is your choice. Our members should have a right to feel that their conversations are respected by the Pastor. They have the right to feel that their money is being used for the purpose it was donated. The majority of the board has made their decision. Helena, if you plan to leave the church instead of remaining as an assistant Pastor, please let us know. We will be changing the locks and security code because we don't want Grace to enter without other people being present. If we give you the right to enter, I know you will pass it on to her. You both have proven yourselves to be untrustworthy. I'm the perfect example. Isn't that right, Violet?"

Violet didn't speak. Lisette sat in silence. Lottie continued, "Are there any other matters before the board that need to be addressed? If not, then this meeting is concluded."

Helena and Grace stormed out. Paul asked, "Do you think someone should spend the night in the church until we get the locks and code changed?"

197

FLAWED DECISIONS MURDER

Lottie answered, "I can get the codes changed today. I'm willing to spend the night. Even though they have a key, if they attempt to come in, the alarm will sound. I will be fine."

Lisette suggested, "Why don't we take shifts spending the day with you, Lottie. I will stay for a while and go over the materials in the office. Richard can bring us dinner and then stay for a while."

Violet called her father to let them know they were done with the meeting. Grey said, "I think we need to talk. There have been a lot of surprises here."

Violet met Grey and Bob at her home. Violet started, "Helena and Grace were voted out of their positions in the church. The majority of the board and church members are in agreement with us. Maybe now, Bob, you can get Lisette to sign off on your paperwork to become an Assistant Pastor. What surprises do you have for me?"

Bob was sitting next to Violet on the couch. "Your father told me he expects that he'll succumb to his illness in only a few weeks. I told your father about how much I cared about you. I was afraid he would worry about you being alone." Bob slid to the floor on one knee, "I asked for his permission to request your hand in marriage." Violet was in shock. She didn't speak or react. Bob said, "I was hoping for a more positive response."

198

MIA TENROC

Violet asked her father, "What did you tell him when he asked?"

Grey answered, "I told him I would neither approve nor disapprove because I didn't know him. That decision, my daughter, is yours. It is good to know that you have friends. That Lottie woman I met today seems very nice. It is good to know that Bob feels so much for you, too. I would recommend that you not hurry. I will be looking down on you from above. I will see your wedding even if I am no longer on Earth. Do what your heart tells you."

Violet turned to Bob, "I am flattered but also surprised. I will say yes to being engaged. We can discuss a marriage later. There is so much on my mind with my father's suffering that I can't rejoice right now."

Bob hugged her, "Of course, that is understandable. I'm not trying to overwhelm you or push you. It does my heart good to know your father understands my honorable intentions."

199

Story

Chapter 43 – The High

Lisette left after they had dinner. Richard stayed to keep Lottie company. "Lottie, I don't mind spending the night here instead of you. You would be more comfortable at home."

Lottie replied thoughtfully, "Actually, tonight I would be more comfortable here. I'm glad we have a chance to be alone. I wanted to talk to you. With Lisette becoming the lead Pastor, she will have some decisions to make. It will also add pressure to your marriage. I know you have a lot of influence with your wife. I wanted to discuss some important matters with you."

Lottie's phone rang. It was Violet. "My father is suffering tonight. We were wondering if we can come to the church for a Native American ceremony. It's not the exact location but it is the best available to us right now. The ceremony will take about 10 hours."

Lottie replied, "Of course, come on over. I will be here all night and I would welcome the company." Lottie turned to Richard. "Violet and her father want to use the church for a ceremony. I won't be alone after all. Before you leave, I will tell you something in confidence. Please promise you won't tell anyone else yet, not even Lisette."

Richard answered, "I don't like keeping secrets from my wife, but you seem very desperate to have someone to talk to. Please go ahead."

Lottie went into full detail about Helena and Grace's trap. She then followed up with the scenario involving Zack and Bob. Richard left with deep concern. He would never had left if it wasn't for Violet and her father coming.

Lottie was very surprised to see Bob in the car with Violet and her father. She would never have agreed to them coming had she known he would be with them. She didn't know how to get out of it now. Violet came in and gave her a hug. "Thank you so much for permitting us to come. I know this church isn't licensed to use the drugs involved in the ceremony but it is a church of the spirits. Father needs to contact those that went before him."

FLAWED DECISIONS MURDER

Lottie tried to assure herself that everything was okay. After all, she didn't believe Bob was aware that she knew about his lies. She had erased the phone call from his son. She would be safe for now, especially with Violet present. Violet asked, "Can you two please wait in the fellowship hall? I need to speak to my father alone."

Lottie tried to hide her fear. "Bob, did you have dinner? There is still some food left from the luncheon."

Bob was watching her with a hard stare. "We ate a little while ago. Thanks, but I'm not hungry. You know this ceremony involves using peyote, right? I'm not going to participate because it is best to have someone that isn't high in case there is an emergency. You are welcome to participate if you like."

Lottie confessed, "I never use drugs or alcohol. I prefer to always be in control."

Bob smiled and moved closer, "That's your problem. You never relax or unwind. It would do you good." Bob left with the excuse of using the men's room, which was located between the chapel and the fellowship hall. He was maneuvering to hear what was being said between Grey and Violet. Lottie took this opportunity to text Richard that Bob was there. She waited but got no respond back.

MIA TENROC

In the next room, Grey was speaking to his daughter. "I never said yes or no to Bob when he asked if he could propose to you. In truth, I don't know him, but I also don't trust him. He doesn't seem to be honest. I can't give you my blessing but I won't think less of you if you choose to proceed. You know him better than I do. That is why you have to make your own decision. I take it from your reaction to the proposal that you aren't very excited about the idea."

Violet confessed, "I can see he really desires Lisette. I think he likes being with me but I'm his second choice. It was wrong of Bob to use Lottie, not only for a home and to support him, but to give her false hope of being in a relationship with him. I enjoy myself when we are together. Bob acts differently when we are alone. I think he is content when he is with me but I don't feel that is enough for a successful marriage. I think the fact that I will inherit your business is adding to his newfound longing to be with me. For right now, I don't care if he says we are engaged, because it is flattering to be wanted. I won't hurry into marriage until I'm sure he sincerely wants me."

Lottie was trying to hurry into the chapel in order to not be alone with Bob. When she rounded the corner, she saw him eavesdropping on the conversation. She backed away quietly. At first, she wasn't going to warn Violet about Bob's bad side, but

FLAWED DECISIONS MURDER

now she realized there was no choice. Violet called out right then, "We are ready to begin. It is up to you if you want to participate."

Lottie used that as an excuse to go into the chapel. It was a long night. Lottie was determined not to fall asleep. Violet smoked some of the peyote while Grey took it in powder form. Bob spent a lot of time in the fellowship hall. Lottie stayed in the chapel with them, but was disappointed that she could not have the conversation with Violet due to her trance-like state.

Around 3:00 a.m., Lottie started to feel sleepy. She had to walk by Bob to go to the fellowship hall. "I'm going to get some coffee if you want to sit with them for a while." Bob nodded yes. Lottie was glad to be alone as she poured out her coffee, to which she added cream and sugar. After drinking a cup, she started to make herself another when suddenly, she began to vomit. She knew that throwing up was a normal reaction after ingesting peyote. She said to herself, "How did that get in me?" It dawned on her that Bob has been in the kitchen the whole time. He must have put the drug in either the cream or the sugar! Lottie fell to the floor.

Bob carried Lottie to the chapel and laid her on the pew with a pillow under her head. "Enjoy your trip," he said. He then took pictures of her to use as

MIA TENROC

blackmail in case Lottie to keep her from telling the truth about Zack.

About 5:00 a.m., Grey and Violet were ready to go. Bob left to drive them home, telling Lottie he would be back. Walking out the door, Bob tried to set the alarm but it didn't work. He went back in the chapel and asked Lottie for the new code. Still high on the peyote, she only comprehended the word "Code", and started muttering the numbers, not realizing she was giving them to Bob. He secured the church and left.

At 8:00 a.m., Lisette walked into the church, carrying breakfast for Lottie. "Odd," she thought, "The door is unlocked. The alarm isn't set." She called out, "Lottie, are you here?" Lisette looked into the fellowship hall. It was empty. She set the meal on the table and walked into the chapel. She let out a blood-curdling scream when she saw Lottie hanging from the church chandelier.

Abletown

Chapter 44 – Interviews

"Nick!" Peter Cranbert shouted as if he had just seen his best friend. "So very good to see you. Who is this young lady with you?"

Nick could tell that Janice was fuming. "This is *Detective* Janice Hoover, my partner. We were wondering if we could speak to you for a few minutes."

Peter laughed, "Wait, I thought Jean was your partner." This only made Janice's ire rise to a new level. "Anyways, I figured that you might be coming here to help with my campaign. I don't know why Jean is supporting the other side."

Janice said sternly, "We need to speak in private, please. If you have a question for Jean, I'm sure she

MIA TENROC

would prefer that you speak directly to her." Nick suppressed his chuckle. Peter was definitely on the wrong side of Janice.

Peter replied, "I don't keep secrets from my staff."

Nick stepped closer and spoke in a very low voice, "Either in your office privately or we can go downtown."

Peter gasped, "Let's go in my office, then." They walked past Priscilla who overheard Nick's comment. The two detectives nodded a hello but said nothing to her. In his office, Peter asked, "What's so important that we must be so secretive?"

Nick produced a picture of Missy aka Trudy. "Do you know this woman? She was murdered on Saturday the 4th."

Peter was surprised and looked seriously at the picture, "I never saw her in my life. No, I don't know her."

Nick asked, "Then why did your campaign pay her by these money orders every week for the past four weeks?"

Peter picked up the money orders and looked at them. "I admit to buying these money orders but I don't know how they would end up in a dead

207

FLAWED DECISIONS MURDER

woman's account. I tell you again, I don't know this woman."

Janice said, "Let's back up to the money orders. You admit that you purchased them. We have that confirmed at the bank. After you obtained the money orders, what did you do with them?"

Peter replied, "I mailed them to a post office box as instructed."

Nick asked, "Instructed by whom?"

Peter paused, "I don't think I can answer this."

Nick tried again, "If I look into your accounting records, what would I find as the reason listed for the purchase and mailing?"

Peter hesitated, "It was for consulting fees. You're not really going to look through my books, are you, Nick?"

Nick replied, "This woman was murdered. You are paying her each week for consulting yet you claim that you never saw her before. How can you explain her doing consultation work for you?"

Peter stood up. "I think I need to consult a lawyer. This is confusing me. I've never seen her before. I did see the story on the news today and it says that she was murdered on the 4th. I was at a campaign speaking engagement that day and went

MIA TENROC

home afterwards. My wife was with me the whole time. She can vouch for me for the entire day. I didn't kill that woman. Please leave."

Nick asked, "Are you going to talk to us after you speak to an attorney?"

Peter quietly said, "I don't know."

Nick pulled out a warrant, "We will need to take your books with us for now. We will make a copy for you so you can continue your work uninterrupted. I like that you are going to see an attorney. This is an awfully serious matter."

They left Peter's office and walked two blocks to the east and then one block north to enter Leon Pierre's office. Again, they were warmly greeted. Leon lead them into his office and shut the door.

Nick began, "Leon, did you know that this woman that worked in your office was murdered?" Leon looked at the picture and nodded. "Do you want an attorney present?"

Leon looked surprised, "You aren't arresting me, are you?"

Nick responded, "No. I know about her coming on to you naked on the day she died. I also know she was alive when you walked away."

209

FLAWED DECISIONS MURDER

Leon looked surprised, "How do you know all that? Something tells me that Jean is involved. She sent a message to me, through Belinda, not to let that woman in my office again. I didn't realize the event you speak of was common knowledge. In a small town like this, that news would make the grapevine fast."

Nick assured him, "Four of us were in Moss Park. Jean was alone on the lookout tower and the rest of us were down below. She saw the whole thing through the viewfinders. The time ran out after you pushed her away and turned to go to your car."

Leon let out a deep breath, "I'm so glad Jean saw it. She can tell you that I didn't accept nor encourage those sexual advances. I'm a normal man. When Missy would flirt with me in the office, I would smile and maybe puff out my chest a little. While I love and am only interested in my wife, it is nice to think a younger woman finds me attractive. Being flattered and being interested are two different things. It was only an ego boost; I was never interested in Missy."

Janice wanted to move the questioning along. "Do you have any information that could be helpful about her death? Did she try to call or contact you after you left?" Leon said she had not. "We think she died shortly after the incident. Did you see anyone

210

MIA TENROC

else around your cabin or on the road?" Leon indicated no.

Nick laid the big news on him. "Did you know that Missy was being paid by Peter's re-election campaign?"

Leon sat up straight, "What! You must be kidding me! Peter and I are on opposite sides about one major issue, otherwise I wouldn't even be running. I retired to this beautiful quiet little town. I don't want to have housing developments next to my home. I thought we were friends except for that issue. Are you saying he paid her to make advances towards me?"

Nick clarified, "Peter claims that he didn't know who she was. I believe him. He didn't have any reaction to the picture. Missy, whose real name was Trudy, was receiving a check from him but I don't believe they ever saw each other. Peter won't tell me why he sent the checks, only that he was told to do so. He is consulting an attorney now. What else can you tell me about her?"

Leon said, "Not much. She showed up in this office one day. She said she agreed with my cause to not permit development of the downtown area and wanted to help on the campaign. I asked if she had a home here, but she never really answered. She replied that she would do anything I requested, like stuff envelopes, make posters, or any other behind-the-

FLAWED DECISIONS MURDER

scene jobs. She said she didn't like to speak in front of people that well. I told her that we already had Belinda for that job. Belinda isn't the campaign manager, but you would never know it. She is great at organizing and speaking to the public. Missy would take calls and give the messages to either Belinda or I to call back. Nothing really outstanding ever happened. She came and worked in the afternoons and left. She never asked for anything or made any special requests. I told Belinda I was going to my cabin to work on a debate coming up with Peter. I like to make sure that I know the facts and figures. I just can't believe Peter would do that to me. Is he that desperate to win?"

Nick suggested, "I would act like nothing happened. If you need to talk to someone, I would trust Belinda. I would say Jean but she is a witness so it would be better not to talk to her, except to say hello if you see her in public. We are not done with the investigation. Right now, we can't even prove that the murder was related to this election except by Jean's gut instincts. You say right now there isn't any gossip about you and Missy so if you don't say anything, maybe it will stay hidden. I can't promise it won't come out. I doubt if Peter will say anything and I know Jean won't. From what Jean just texted me, the murder and the picture of Missy is on the news. That will be all around town but not the encounter at

212

your cabin. We will get back to you as soon as we have any information."

Leon asked, "You don't believe I did it, do you?"

Janice answered, "Did you?"

Leon said, "No."

Nick shook his hand, "I really don't believe you did. I hope I'm right. I do think you have a very stormy road ahead. I also suggest not contacting Peter until we get this cleared up."

Abletown

Chapter 45 – Unjustified

Jean was leading the afternoon water aerobics with Josephine, Belinda, Eve and Gwen in the pool. Priscilla stormed in, "How dare you!"

Jean looked surprised, "Gwen might be in your usual spot but there is still room in the pool, if you want to join us."

Priscilla was almost in tears, "What kind of person are you? Sending your policeman boyfriend, husband, or whatever he is, to harass Peter. Why are you playing dirty? He took our accounting books. You put him up to it, I know it!"

Jean was only half as mad as Josephine. Her sister leaped to her defense. "Do you really believe that Jean would do something so underhanded, or that

MIA TENROC

her boyfriend would risk losing his position after over 20 years with the police force to play some kind of game?"

Belinda interjected, "When does anyone tell Nick what to do? He is a good man. You have no need to attack either him or Jean." Eve and Jean were silent. They knew why the accounting books were taken. They probably would be evidence.

Josephine was coming out of the pool, "You need to leave now. If you don't want to act like a friend or good person, then please stay away from us. That's what you've already chosen to do. You turned your back on your friends for someone that doesn't even know you exist or give you the time of day." Priscillas stormed out as Josephine got back into the pool.

Jean looked close to tears. "I hate it that our friendship has ended. Even if she tried to rejoin us, I would always be nice to her, but it would take a lot for that trust to ever return."

Josephine turned to her sister, "Why would Nick take the accounting books? Do you know?" Eve looked guilty. Josephine turned to address her, "You know. I can tell."

Jean said quietly. "We are witnesses. We can't discuss the case. I'm sorry. I don't mean to keep secrets. I will tell you as soon as Nick says I can."

FLAWED DECISIONS MURDER

Belinda smiled, "We know you would. We didn't mean to apply pressure or make you feel guilty."

Rosie, who lived two apartments from Jean at the home and loved to gossip, came running to the pool. "I just came from the bank. The teller said the police were there to ask about some money orders that Peter purchased but that the manager of the branch won't tell them anything about it. Do any of you know what's going on?"

Josephine and Belinda looked at each other. They just got the answer to their questions. Josephine answered, "No, not a thing. Keep us informed if you hear anything."

Rosie said chipperly, "Right! Will do!" Then she ran from the area to spread the gossip.

Jean said, "Please don't even try to guess. I don't want to confirm or deny anything."

Right then, numerous cell phones rang and indications of voicemail messages being left filled the air. With the women being wet and in the middle of exercise, the calls would need to wait until they were done. Belinda was the first one out of the pool and looking at her phone. "Leon is wanting me to come over. He says it's extremely important. He wondered if you could come too, Jean."

MIA TENROC

Jean declined, "I think it is best if I don't talk to either of the candidates. I'm a witness to the war they are waging."

Eve said, "Peter is wanting me to come to Mr. Manor's office. I think I will hurry over."

Josephine stated, "Fannie is wanting to know what is going on. She wondered if we can go back to her store."

Jean suggested, "Why don't you go over and find out what the town gossip is saying. It might be important news for Eve and Belinda so they can tell their candidates how to proceed. Sometimes the word in town needs to be ignored and other times the gossip needs to be addressed and corrected." Looking at her phone, she said, "It looks like Nick and Janice want to meet me for dinner."

Gwen observed, "Looks like you four work as a team supervising the town."

Jean smiled, "I hope not in a negative way." She was about to call Nick back when he came through the door. "Why don't you and Janice come here for dinner. I can get the kitchen to make a few plates and we can eat in my room."

Nick agreed, "It's probably best to avoid the questions that we would be asked if we ate at the local

FLAWED DECISIONS MURDER

diner. Belinda, I was wondering if we could talk for a few minutes."

Belinda explained, "I was just headed over to Leon's campaign headquarters. He sounds desperate right now."

Nick smiled, "I bet he does feel shocked and needs direction, but this will only take a few minutes." The others left and Nick started his discussion. He asked questions about what Belinda observed with Leon and his interaction with Missy. He asked about Missy's duties: what she said, did, and her communications with the others in the campaign.

Belinda said, "I feel like I'm betraying Leon when I said he was flattered by the attention Missy gave him. He never once made an inappropriate action toward her."

Nick inquired, "Do you know anything about Peter's campaign or workers?"

Belinda responded, "No. I only know that they are loyal to him. Priscilla is to the point of turning her back on her friends. At least Jean's stories are a distraction. We don't want to think about what is happening in our own town."

Story

Chapter 46 – Lisette and Richard

Lisette tried to think about what to do. She pulled out her cell phone and called 911, then telling her name and location. She explained, "I walked to the body and touched Lottie. She is cold and unresponsive. Her spirit has left the body. I backed out without touching anything else. I would have taken her down to do CPR but didn't feel like there was any hope. Should I go in and try to see if she can be revived?"

The voice on the phone told her. "It would be better to leave the crime scene as it is. Please leave the church and wait in your car until we arrive. It will only be minutes, I promise. Officers are in the neighborhood and are already in route."

FLAWED DECISIONS MURDER

Lisette did as she was told. She started to cry. Her body was shaking. "I need to call my husband. I'm about to lose control. I feel faint. I'm sitting in my car. I see the police car headed this way. Can I hang up now and call my husband?" The voice approved the action. Before she could call, the officer walked to her car. Lisette explain the situation and the officers told her to stay in the car and to wait for them to return. They then hurried to the door. Lisette called Richard and said in a sobbing voice. "Lottie is dead! I got to the church and went inside to see her hanging from the chandelier. I called the police and they arrived in minutes and are in there now. Please come quickly!"

Richard responded, "I'm on my way. Are you ok?" Lisette continued to cry. She was in shock.

The detectives arrived, as did the tech team. After a review of the scene, Detective Bishop asked Lisette to go with her to a bench in a small garden area at the side of the church. "I don't want you to go inside the church until we have a chance to go over every area. I hope you don't mind sitting outside. I understand you are the pastor of the church, is that correct?"

Lisette insisted that Richard be permitted to join them. Richard supplied the answer. "Lisette was voted to become head pastor yesterday afternoon. She was the assistant pastor before that. Helena was the head

MIA TENROC

pastor for the past 20 years, ever since her sister died. Her sister founded the church."

Detective Bishop knew immediately this was the first line of questioning. "Lisette, would you like to tell me what happened."

Lisette tried but could hardly speak. "My husband knows those facts. Please permit him to answer for me."

Richard brought a box of tissues with him. He handed them over to his wife, while he continued. "Helena is a negative person sometimes. Her daughter, Grace, was taking money from the church funds. Only a few hundred here and there. Helena and Grace feel this is their church so their actions weren't inappropriate. Lottie was the head of the committee that oversaw the running of the church. Each year, we vote for the person to lead the various offices in the church. Yesterday, they voted that my wife become the head pastor but allowed Helena to remain as the assistant. They also voted that Grace could no longer be the bookkeeper. Another person was elected to that position. Both Helena and Grace were so angry that Lottie was afraid they would come in and destroy the records of the church. Lottie changed the alarm code but we couldn't get a locksmith to come until this morning. In fact, we didn't think to call and he is

221

FLAWED DECISIONS MURDER

pulling in the driveway now. Should I go handle it and tell him to come back later?"

Bishop thought, "See if he can come back later today. Since the potential suspects have a key, it might be a good idea to change the locks. We want time to cover all aspects of the crime scene before he does any changes." Richard left to follow her instructions. "Lisette, do you think that Helena or Grace would murder over losing their positions in the church?"

Lisette thought. "I don't like to think bad about anyone. I do know they were very mad and hurt after the vote. I can see them contacting church and board members to contest the vote, but murder seems a bit drastic."

Richard returned so the next question was for either to answer. "Did Lottie have any other enemies? Can you tell me as much as possible about her?"

Richard answered, "Lisette, maybe you won't want to hear the next thing I have to say. Do you want me to talk to the detective alone?"

Lisette responded, "No. I want to hear what is said. I know I'm overreacting to the loss of my friend. This was the first time something like this has ever happened to me. I can handle the truth and I want to know it."

MIA TENROC

Richard put his arm around her but looked and talked to Detective Bishop. "There is one other person that you might want to check into. His name is Bob. He was living with Lottie but not in a romantic way. Lottie at first wanted him. She was single and looking for a husband. Bob can be quite the charmer. Bob came to this church as a broken man. He said his son, Zack, was ill and that chances are he wouldn't live much longer. Lottie talked to his son on Saturday night and found out that was all a lie. Bob took the boy when he was 2 years old and had been living off the grid for 10 years. He told his son that the mother died. The boy found out later that was a lie. He called the mother, and she came to get him. Lottie said when the phone rang, she was afraid it was an emergency and thus answered. She asked about Zack's health and said she would get Bob out of the shower. Because of the panic in her voice, Zack told her there was nothing wrong with his health. They talked and Lottie found out that Bob was telling all of us a lie. Zack told her how to go in and delete the call so Bob wouldn't know it had occurred. He then made Lottie swear not to tell anyone. Bob was trying to become a pastor, but Helena didn't like him and wouldn't sign off on the paperwork. Bob was leading the attack on Helena through other people, like Lottie. Lottie realized that Bob should not become a leader in the church after finding out the truth. However, we all agreed that

FLAWED DECISIONS MURDER

Helena should go no matter what was occurring with Bob. She wasn't a person we trusted either. She would divulge confidences and permit the stealing of the funds. I feel you should check into Bob as a suspect as well."

Lisette looked shocked. "I find that hard to believe about Bob. He seemed so sincere and concerned for his son."

Richard looked at his wife, "Did you ever notice that Bob is obsessed with you? He becomes sexually aroused whenever you sing. He is a very cunning man. Bob is very good looking and knows how to manipulate people around him. Whenever he tells the stories about his son, you give him hugs and comfort. I have no clue why Bob told the lie to begin with, but he never mentions his son except when he is alone with you. Did you also notice that there was no talk about replacing Helena before he came? He likes to get his way and will use anyone around him to get it."

Lisette looked sad, "I thought maybe it was because he is a private person and didn't want to tell the story of his son to everyone. Why would Lottie tell you this?"

Richard looked at his wife, "I'm sure the police will find out if it is true or not. Lottie didn't know what to do with the information. She didn't want to ruin Bob's hopes and dreams if it wasn't true. She felt

MIA TENROC

convinced that Zack was being honest. She told me last night in confidence because she wanted me to help her in delaying the signature on the paperwork that would make Bob a leader in this church. She knew you would talk to me about it before you signed. Lottie said something that really made me proud. She said that she felt I could be trusted with the secret and that I would help investigate before you signed the paperwork." Richard turned to the detective. "Lottie was a good person. She tried hard to do what was right. I'm glad she felt she could trust me. I wouldn't have told you the secret, but I feel it might be important to the case. My wife and I spent the day with Lottie in the church to protect the records. We suggested taking them home but Lottie wanted to be away from Bob. Violet and her father were coming over to spend the night in the church so I felt it would be safe to leave. Lottie texted me that Bob had showed up with them. She felt it was safe because Bob didn't know that she knew his secret."

Story

Chapter 47 – Violet and Grey

Detective Bishop got the information from Richard and Lisette about Lottie's employment, financial background, and social life. Quick checks were performed by her partner to prove that it was true. Lottie lead a good life. She had casual friends, but no best buddies. Lottie didn't date anyone, and had little social life. She didn't drink nor go to parties. Bishop also got the information available on Bob and Violet.

Detective Bishop and her partner, Detective Robinson, went to Violet's apartment. It was a very unusual scene. There was music playing with Native American chanting. Violet explained, "My father is dying. It could be as soon as today. Last night, we did a ceremony to see our elders that passed before us.

MIA TENROC

Now he is in bed and we are playing the traditional music. It is not right that none of our people are present for this ceremony, but there are not many from our tribe in the area. Why are the police here? Is it to arrest my father and myself?"

Detective Bishop explained, "I'm sorry but I have bad news. Lottie died at the church this morning."

Both Violet and Bob looked surprised. Bob was especially upset. "What happened? I live at Lottie's house and we are very good friends. We just left her a few hours ago and she was asleep on one of the pews in the church. She was fine when we left."

Robinson asked, "What time did you leave the church?"

Bob replied, "It was 5:00 a.m."

Robinson continued to question, "Did you lock the door? Did you set the alarm?"

Bob almost shouted when he said, "Of course I did." He started to tear slightly but refused to cry. "I thought it would be ok. Grey was weak and felt a need to get home and to bed. I knew Richard or Lisette would be bringing breakfast soon. She was sleeping so peacefully. Why didn't I stay or wake her to come with us?"

Detective Bishop went into the room where Grey was resting. He greeted her. "The white doctors said 3

FLAWED DECISIONS MURDER

weeks to 3 months to live. I came to be with my only child so she would know what to do for me to have a safe crossing. I also want to confer with her about the running of the business and deliver proper paperwork. If I knew the end was so soon, I would have had her come to me in Oklahoma so I would be with my people. Now, I'm destined to die in a strange place. I did the ceremony last night. I admit to using peyote at the church last night. It is our way. If there is any trouble, you need to blame it on me."

Detective Bishop assured Grey, "I'm not here because of that. I too have Native American blood in me. I too can see spirits. You did what was right and what you had to. There will be no trouble."

As they talked, Grey seemed to gain a little strength. He asked, "Why are the police here then? Lottie seemed very nice. I didn't know her before but since she is a leader in the church, she said we could do our ceremony there. Due to the pain, I was very out of it. Lottie seemed a little out of it herself even though she declined to participate in the service. It seemed odd to me. I was so sick that Bob had to carry me to the car. I hope to regain enough strength that my daughter can drive me home. I hope that can happen."

Bishop reached a reassuring hand to rest on his shoulder. "I hope you regain your strength enough,

MIA TENROC

too. Did Bob or your daughter participate in the ceremony?"

Grey felt comfort with Bishop. "My daughter did to a degree. Bob did not. Lottie said she wouldn't but I believe she too had peyote. She was sick at her stomach and was clearly reaching to another world."

Bishop asked, "When you left, did Bob or Violet lock the door? Did Lottie know you were leaving?"

Grey had a sad look in his eyes. "She was such a nice person. I believe she was asleep on the pew. It was a long night. I really can't be certain. I don't remember much except Bob lifting me." He turned and was falling asleep so Bishop patted his shoulder, whispered a thank you, and quietly left the room.

Violet entered the room to check on her father. After seeing he was resting comfortably, she came out of the room to ask the detectives, "What is next? Are we in some trouble?"

Bishop instructed, "We want to interview you and Bob. Bob, you will take much longer since your relationship was very close with Lottie. It would be best not to do it here since Grey needs quiet and rest. Do you think we can come into Lottie's house and look around? I will speak with Violet a few minutes, then join you and Detective Robinson outside. Afterwards, we can go to the house."

229

FLAWED DECISIONS MURDER

Bob suddenly realized there was more to this investigation. "How did Lottie die? Why are you wanting to search her house? What aren't you telling us? Was Lottie's death of natural causes?"

Bishop, keeping her voice calm and matter-of-fact, answered, "We don't know yet. We are trying to determine if it was suicide or murder."

Bob reacted with anger, "I don't believe for a minute that Lottie would commit suicide. She was sad because she hadn't found her life mate, but overall she was a happy person."

Bob was willing to stay outside while the interview with Violet occurred. Bishop asked, "You seem upset but not to a large degree. Were you and Lottie friends?"

Violet started to tear up. "This is so hard. It seems too much for me to handle, first all that my father is going through and now hearing the news of Lottie. I didn't know Lottie well. I saw her around church, but we never talked. I recently joined the committee she led and much has happened since then. I was very upset over my father. I don't have many friends here. Bob plays in a band. He asked me to join him at the clubs to hear him play. I thought he was just being friendly because of my situation. I have been very depressed. I went to the clubs just to keep my mind from thinking about my problems. I thought

230

MIA TENROC

Lottie was interested in Bob, but I didn't know for sure. There was nothing between Bob and I. We weren't dating and there was no romance. On Friday, Helena and Grace convinced Lottie to go to the club where Bob was playing. I figured she got the wrong idea about us so I called her in the morning and asked to meet for lunch. That was now two days ago. We talked and she said she wasn't interested in Bob, and I told her I wasn't interest in that way either. We became friends fast. I liked her. We were both upset over Helena and Grace trying to cause a fight between us. We agreed to band together to keep Helena from being such a bad person to her church members. Instead of dividing us, we stood united when we voted her out."

Violet started to cry. Bishop said, "I'm sorry this is so hard on you. Lottie sounded like a nice person. Do you have any other information that could help? Did she ever mention other boyfriends or problems at work?"

Violet shook her head no. "The lunch, the meeting, and last night were really the only times we talked. We were on the same page. I really hoped the friendship would grow."

"Bob said he carried your father to the car this morning. Did you walk to the car on your own? Did you see Bob lock the door and set the alarm?"

231

FLAWED DECISIONS MURDER

Violet thought. "I was a little out of it too. It was a long night. I did walk to the car on my own. After Bob put my father in the passenger seat, I covered him with a blanket. I went around and climbed into the little backseat space behind the driver side. Bob did walk to the door and I did see him put in a key and turn the lock. He did touch the keypad, but I don't know if the alarm was set or not." Feeling like she was putting in the kiss of death, Violet confessed, "I was honest when I told you there was nothing between Bob and I. That was my perception. I think Bob might feel differently. He asked my father for my hand in marriage. We didn't have a chance to talk about it until last night at the church. Bob and Lottie were not in the sanctuary with us. My father told me that he told Bob he would respect my choice. Father told me in private that he didn't trust Bob. There was no reason but just an instinct. I am sure neither Bob nor Lottie heard the conversation but if they did, it could have a bearing on what happened."

Abletown

Chapter 48 – A Deal

"Oh, my goodness," said Belinda. "That was a shocker. Violet must have felt terrible telling on Bob. Of course, we have our own mystery here. Eve, can you throw Peter under the bus? What happened when you went to talk to Mr. Manor yesterday?"

Eve actually backed away, "No way will I tell! What was said in the room was in confidence. Basically, Mr. Manor asked me some questions, since I'm an accountant, to do with finances. I answered the questions but didn't say anything I didn't have to."

Josephine laughed at Eve. "So basically, you're not saying anything about not saying anything?" Eve looked confused with the logic but said nothing. Josephine continued, "So what else aren't you telling

FLAWED DECISIONS MURDER

us? You don't look dressed for tea at Fannie's nor for water aerobics."

Eve made her excuses, "I have lunch plans today, and then I'm going for a ride on a motorcycle."

Jean's eyebrow raised, "Your transportation doesn't count as a motorcycle. It is a scooter. That is, unless you are riding on another vehicle."

Eve blushed, "If you must know, Connor and I are going to have a bite to eat at my place. He needs a special part for his motorcycle, and Nigel happens to have what he needs. We are going out to the farm to dig through my husband's junk." All the ladies looked stunned. Eve justified, "There is nothing romantic going on between Connor and me. We do enjoy each other's company. It's not like Nigel acts interested anymore, other than that I'm his meal ticket. It's nice to have someone to enjoy lunch with occasionally. It's nice to have a man who listens when I talk. Connor and I laugh a lot and have fun. I won't say what would happen if I were single and younger. Connor wants to marry again and have children. Both won't happen in a relationship with me. Don't worry, I know what I'm doing."

Jean, Belinda, and Josephine walked to Fannie's place. Jean said under her breath, "I hope she does. This sounds like a tricky situation. Eve sure looks interested in Connor to me."

MIA TENROC

Fannie greeted them with, "Did you hear the latest news? You probably already know, Jean."

Jean looked surprised, "What do I know about?"

Fannie put her hands on her hips, "Like Nick didn't tell you? Mr. Manor and Peter Cranbert left town early this morning for a meeting. We are sure that it was with Nick because Eddie Jacob was at the county buildings pulling a permit for construction of a shed in his backyard. He saw the three of them talking and then they walked into the police station."

Jean defended Nick, "Nick doesn't tell me anything about his work. He could lose his job for that. I know nothing about a meeting." Jean then picked up her phone and sent a text to Nick.

Fannie asked, "Where is Eve? She might know what's going on." Belinda told about Eve's plans to take Connor to buy a motorcycle part from Nigel. Fannie raised her eyebrows, just like Jean had done, "I don't think it's a good idea to let the boytoy meet the husband."

Nick was sitting at his desk when Jean's text arrived. He chuckled and put the phone down. Janice looked at him. "What's so funny?"

Nick replied, "Jean. She is fishing for information. She asked if I was going to be in Abletown today."

235

FLAWED DECISIONS MURDER

"How is that fishing?" asked Janice.

"The investigation calls for us to be in Abletown. We would be there now if it wasn't for Mr. Manor and Mr. Cranbert coming to us. Jean is smart enough to know that. I would bet that the town gossip is the two of them driving out of town together. If we aren't in Abletown, Jean will assume that this is where the two men went."

Janice looked up to see the DA representative arrive. "Do you really think she figured all that out? Here is the DA. Maybe now we can get answers to our questions from Peter Cranbert." Janice stood and welcomed Mr. Smith from the DA office. "The men are waiting in the conference room. Please follow me."

Settled in the room, Mr. Cranbert kept reiterating, "I want assurance that I will not be arrested or prosecuted for anything I'm about to tell you. I'm an innocent man. I have done nothing wrong. I'm here to cooperate with a police investigation. I need you to tell me that you understand this."

Mr. Smith replied, "I can't give you that guarantee until I know what you did." This conversation continued to the point that the two men were getting short-tempered. "Mr. Cranbert, do not waste my time. I need to know the facts before I can give you the assurance you seek."

236

MIA TENROC

Nick interrupted, "How about I tell you what I think Mr. Cranbert might say, and then you can say that if that is the fact, we will work with you." All eyes were on Nick as he continued, "Modern Change Builders is wanting to tear down most of Abletown and put in modern buildings. I believe it would be large tall buildings with stores on the bottom floor and condos in the upper levels. Most of the town is very opposed to the change."

Mr. Smith glared, "What does that have to do with anything?"

Nick smiled, "Hundreds of millions of dollars can create a cause for murder. Peter feels he hasn't been paid properly for all he did for the town over the years, in spite of knowing the salary when he ran for the position. Not working a second job, he now finds he doesn't have enough saved for retirement. This election is based on one issue. If Peter gets in, he will help push against the ordinance that keeps the builders from doing the development, in exchange he will be rewarded with an income in some way. Leon Pierre is running because he retired there and doesn't want the town destroyed."

Peter spoke up, "'Destroyed' is a bit extreme. The town needs to grow and change to keep up with the world."

FLAWED DECISIONS MURDER

Nick ignored him and continued, "Modern Change Builders are contributing to Mr. Cranbert's campaign through a pact to keep from being directly linked to him. The company is giving him instructions on what to do. Peter is to take part of the funds and pay a 'consultant' and a photographer. Peter was instructed to take the money and obtain money orders and mail them to the two people. He has never seen nor spoke to them. At least, that is true of the consultant. Peter doesn't realize that he was paying a prostitute who was working at Leon's headquarters. Her job was to seduce Leon and get damaging photos of him. Those photos would have been released just before the election. Abletown has a population with a high moral code and believes in proper conduct. The photos would've repulsed the voters who would have prioritized the scandal over the building issue. Peter will tell you he didn't know that was the plan. The builders ran the money through Peter instead of paying it directly to the two people because they wanted Peter to be trapped. If he doesn't come through with his promise, the company will have the ability to expose Peter to the public. Peter now realizes he is in a trap and that is why he is wanting to make a deal. If these are the facts, would you realize he isn't evil but more of a fool and not charge him with a crime? One more thing, the person hired to

MIA TENROC

discredit Leon is now dead. Missy aka Trudy Must has been murdered."

Mr. Manor started to laugh. "How do you know that whole story?"

Nick smiled, "Let's just say a little birdie told me."

Peter glared, "You mean Jean, the person that has her hand in everything in town."

Mr. Smith looked at Nick, "Is he talking about Jean, your girlfriend, wife, or whatever you call your relationship?"

Janice answered, "Jean was already aware that Mr. Cranbert was involved in the picture scheme before she knew Trudy was dead. When interviewing witnesses, we learned Jean had already talked to them. We talked to Jean, who provided us with the information she obtained, and then she dropped her investigation because she didn't want to interfere with the police. She is no longer involved except as a witness."

Peter looked defeated. "How did Jean know what was going on when I didn't?"

Nick looked pleasant but with a cutting tone said, "The money didn't mess up her vision. You do realize Jean's three times Great-Grandfather John Satterthwaite built four of the houses that could

239

FLAWED DECISIONS MURDER

potentially get destroyed, including his original homestead. Your building for the future would destroy an important part of Josephine and Jean's past."

Peter admitted, "Everything Nick said was true. I was actually told to go purchase the money orders from another town. I didn't see the need to do that, and purchased the money orders at the local bank. I entered every dime correctly into the accounting books. The checks were made payable to cash, like I was instructed to do, but with the entry labeled payment for the consultant and the photographer. I stapled my copy of the money order to the page with the entry. I'm not trying to hide anything, except the deal I made with the developers."

Mr. Smith stood, "At a state level, I see no criminal wrongdoing since your deal hasn't been completed. You took steps to do something wrong but haven't completed the act. I suggest you tell Janice and Nick everything you know." Mr. Smith walked out the door.

Nick and Janice started the many questions that only Mr. Cranbert could provide the answers to in order to find their killer.

Abletown

Chapter 49 – Peter Comes Clean

Nick began the questions, "I need to know all you can tell me about the photographer. Have you ever seen him or had contact with him?

Peter sighed, "I did meet him once. He came to the office and took photos of me. He sent them to me by regular mail on a jump drive so I could upload them and use them for publicity. I don't have contact information except a Post Office box number. Here is the information where I sent his payments. I thought it was odd that he didn't come and take pictures of me at events, especially with what I was paying him. He never told me a name other than the Dan Greene that I made the checks to. I looked him up online and never found him listed. I did think it was really odd that a photographer wouldn't want to be known."

FLAWED DECISIONS MURDER

Janice asked, "Can you tell us exactly what was said on the one meeting? Try to do it word for word as much as possible."

Peter thought, "It was September 23. He was sitting in my office at the campaign headquarters when I arrived. The girls said he just walked in and asked to see me. He told them that he was hired to take pictures for me. I walked in and introduced myself. I asked him who he was and who had hired him. He looked sleezy. I don't know quite how to describe him. He was about 6 foot, about 200 pounds or a little more. He had broad shoulders and a little bit of a beer belly. He was dressed in jeans and a dark plaid flannel shirt. It looked cheap like you could get at any discount store. His dark hair was long and not kept. It was like he hadn't shampooed it for a while and he had a beard that was messy but not long. His eyebrows were bushy and he had dark brown eyes. He didn't smile or act friendly. He said to me that I was the one that sent for him. I tried to say I hadn't, but he said that I had already paid him by money order. That's when I knew that he was hired by the builders."

Janice inquired, "You haven't seen or spoken to him except that one day?"

Peter acted offended. "That's what I told you. I only saw him the one day."

242

MIA TENROC

Janice continued, "Do you have the package that the picture was sent in?"

"No. I didn't see any need to keep that. It was a regular yellow envelope with the bubble padding that you get at any store. There was no return address. I did notice the post office mark was the one from Central Station where I mailed the checks. I figured it was from him as soon as I saw it."

Nick asked, "Did he say why he wanted photos of you? According to Jean, you are using the publicity photo that you used on our last campaign four year ago on all your fliers and newsletters."

"No. I just did what I was told. I called the builders and they said they sent him but never said why. I asked why I needed a photographer at all and the president of the company, Jamison Bottoms, just laughed and said the word 'insurance'. Now I feel like a fool. Do you think that if I didn't do as they said that they would have doctored the photos to use against me? I thought of that often after that conversation. I went along with the developers because I thought I was getting the money owed to me. I don't deserve getting dragged into a murder investigation."

Nick was getting irritated at Peter's self-pity. "Tell me about the builders. Did they approach you?"

Peter answered, "Of course they came to me. I didn't even think about going to them. This Bottoms

243

FLAWED DECISIONS MURDER

guy called on me at the house. He said he knew I was thinking of retiring but couldn't afford to. He said that if I got the council to approve the building they wanted and if I got the ordinance on historic zoning to fail, they would hire me as a consultant after I retired at $50,000.00 per year. The company bought a piece of land I was looking at that was in the country. They could build me the log cabin of my dreams for free by incorporating the cost of the supplies in the invoices used for the buildings in Abletown. Bottoms said no one would ever know. I didn't care what they did on their paperwork as long as I got the house I wanted. It wasn't my books that would be dishonest. I did call them after you left the office the other day. They said there was nothing to connect them to me on the paperwork. They said there was nothing that you could prove about a connection with the murdered girl. I had an alibi for the time of the murder. They said just to keep my mouth shut and tell no one anything. I don't think he knew about the murder before I called. After I told him, he paused for a very long time. He asked a lot of questions about your visit and what was said. He muted me while I was talking, I think to consult with someone else. I felt uncomfortable doing what he said. I called Mr. Manor at first and talked to him. He told me that by not coming to you, I would be withholding evidence in a murder investigation. I could get in trouble for that

MIA TENROC

even though I knew nothing about the murder itself. I might be wanting to get ahead a little more in life but I'm not a dishonest or evil man."

Nick assured Peter, "I know you're not a bad person. I don't think you realized the problems that could result from your association with the builders. Unfortunately for you, the worst problem that could occur did. You are here to try to make that right. Thank you for coming forward and being honest."

Nick called Jean and invited her to come to the city for dinner. He knew he couldn't discuss the case with her but felt she should be rewarded with a few hints.

That night after dinner, Jean said, "I'm glad that Peter is being cooperative. I did figure he was talking to you. Someone from town saw him enter the station. He's not a bad person but certainly not the brightest. Tomorrow during story time, the friends will hear about a less cooperative person's interview with the police."

245

Story

Chapter 50 – Bob

Detectives Bishop and Robinson suggested that while the research team looked over Lottie's house, that they would take Bob to the police station for their interview. Bob was angry, "I don't mind talking to you but why can't we do it here?"

Bishop explained, "You will probably be providing us with valuable information and I just think it would be better if we could do it on film so that we can refer back to it while we investigate."

"If that is the case, I don't plan to answer questions without a lawyer. I didn't do anything wrong. Lottie was my friend. You are acting like I'm the suspect."

MIA TENROC

Robinson replied, "You say there was nothing in your relationship that was more than friendship but in the case of murder, we must consider the husband, boyfriend, or roommate as a suspect until proven otherwise."

Bob protested, "I was with Grey and Violet the whole time after we left the church and they knew she was fine when we left."

Upon arriving at the police station, an attorney that hung around the station looking for cases, offered to sit with Bob. They talked privately for a while, then consented to the interview. Bob said, "I want to restate for the camera, I didn't kill or hurt Lottie in any way. She was my friend and nothing more. I needed a place to stay and she needed a handyman to help around the house. We never slept together. The only kiss we did was on the cheek like a brother and sister would do."

Robinson asked, "Did Lottie have any boyfriends? Did she date?"

Bob answered, "Not to my knowledge. I never saw her with anybody, nor did she talk about anyone from the present or past."

Bishop asked, "Did she have any enemies at work, at church, or any other social activity?"

247

FLAWED DECISIONS MURDER

Bob looked at his attorney and replied, "Not to my knowledge. She was happy going to work so I assume it was a positive situation. You would have to inquire there. I don't know that she ever went anywhere other than church. She was the head of a committee that does the hiring and firing at the church. The current Pastor Helena was a very mean person. She gossips about things told in confidence. She tried to make people fail. Her daughter, Grace, the bookkeeper, had been caught on more than one occasion taking money from the church and not keeping proper records. Both were relieved of their positions yesterday. If you want a suspect, I would start with them."

Robinson's turn, "Were you instrumental in their dismissal?"

Bob could tell that was a loaded question, "I am not sorry to see them get their just reward. I had no vote. With living in Lottie's home, she was a first-hand witness to Helena's efforts to keep me from getting my pastor license. Lottie talking about ending Helena's rein were the words I wanted to hear so I didn't discourage her."

Bishop asked, "Violet said Grey told her that you asked for her hand in marriage. Is that true?"

MIA TENROC

Bob turned to the attorney and had a whispered discussion, "I don't see why you are asking. What does that have to do with the case?"

Bishop explained, "We don't know yet if Lottie's death was murder or suicide. It could be that Lottie took her own life due to the fact that you chose another. That doesn't make you guilty of murder but it might lead to the answer of her death."

Bob thought, "At first, Lottie did flirt with me. I never led her on. I think my consistent friendship without responding to her flirtation made her realize that we were just friends. She didn't act upset over it. In fact, we hit a comfortable level with each other. I don't think Helena knew that because she set up a meeting where Lottie would see Violet and I together. There was no bad reaction to it. Violet and Lottie seemed even friendlier after the encounter. Lottie was a strong person. Even if she had to deal with hurt, I think she would overcome her problems and move forward. I personally wasn't around to witness it, but I heard she had to deal with losing her parents and that was hard."

Robinson approached the main reason for the taped interview, "It is our understanding that you have a son that has been ill. Was Lottie supportive of your son? Did she have any encounters with him?"

FLAWED DECISIONS MURDER

Bob stopped to think. He asked for private time with his attorney. Bob knew Lottie talked to his son. He wondered if the police knew that. If he lied, then they would doubt everything he said, and he would be even more of a suspect. If he told the truth, that could also make him a suspect because Lottie could've told his secret. When the questioning resumed, he answered the question. "I didn't want to answer you because it would implicate me in a crime. I kidnapped my son 11 years ago. I didn't like being limited to a part-time dad. I loved my son and didn't like answering to my ex on everything. He has returned to living with his mother. She had decided not to prosecute me for the crime. I didn't know if I should confess that to you but my attorney said total honesty was best. I was so upset the day he left. I ran into Pastor Lisette that day for the first time. I couldn't confess what I did, but wanted to talk about the loss I felt with my son leaving. I did lie to her and it got around the church. I never made any comments about him to anyone other than Lisette. I didn't want to add to the lie. I know Lottie knew the truth, even though we never discussed it. To my knowledge, she didn't tell anyone. I can't imagine how you found out but again it isn't an issue. I think Lottie knew me for the good person that I really am. A loving father that put his son above everything. Her knowing the truth wasn't an issue."

MIA TENROC

Bishop changed the direction of the interview. "Tell me what happened when you left the church. Did you set the alarm?"

Bob was glad for the change of topic. "Lottie was lying on the pew. It had been a long night. She said she would participate in the ceremony but she seemed out of it at various times. I can't explain why. I told her that after a little sleep, I was coming back to clean the church. Lottie told me that they had changed the alarm code. She told me the code. I locked the door and set the alarm when I left."

After the interview, Robinson and Bishop compared thoughts. Robinson said, "I think he is lying through his teeth with some truth stuck in. I think he led Lottie on so he could use her for a place to live. I think he may have taken his son, but not because he is a loving father. We need to check that out to be sure. Lottie could have destroyed him, and he knew it. He had motive. Richard said he thought Lottie was afraid of him. That is why she told him the story and let him know Bob showed up with Violet and Grey. I can't prove he did it, but I'm not crossing him off my book."

Bishop agreed. "I can see him doing murder if it suited him. I sure hope Violet knows what kind of man he really is and doesn't get involved with him. I

FLAWED DECISIONS MURDER

wonder why he is after Violet? I don't believe it's love."

Story

Chapter 51 – Helena

Bishop and Robinson tried to contact Helena and Grace at their home but no one was there. Bishop called the phone number that Lisette provided for Helena's cell phone. She did answer. "This is Detective Bishop from the police department. There has been an event at the church and we need to interview you regarding the incident."

Helena sounded surprised, "I'm no longer Senior Pastor. I suggest you contact Lisette. I will give you her number." Bishop assured her she had spoken to Lisette. "What? You already talked to Lisette? I did a quick trip out of town. I'm on the road right now. I will arrive in about two hours. I would be glad to come by the station as soon as I arrive."

FLAWED DECISIONS MURDER

Helena tried to call her daughter. She was very curious about what was going on. "Hi Mom, I hope you are having a good trip."

Helena asked, "What is going on at the church? I had the police call me and want to talk to me."

Grace replied, "I have no clue. I went shopping today and haven't been neither at home nor the church. I told you I would never enter those doors until they do what is right and return you to head pastor."

Helena went to the police station before returning home. The detective took her to an interview room. Helena expressed with confusion and irritation, "What is going on here?"

Bishop explained, "We brought you to the interview room to deliver the bad news in private. Lottie Simmer's body was found in the church this morning. We don't know if it was murder or suicide. Can you tell us anything about her? Did she have any enemies?"

Helena really did look surprised. She held her hand to her chest for a minute. "In spite of the problems we had yesterday, when she led a vote to remove me as Senior Pastor, we were friendly. I have known her for years. I'm so sorry to hear the news. I felt sure that things would've been straightened out soon. Can I have some water, please?" Helena looked

MIA TENROC

small and frail. She took a drink and sat for a minute before continuing, "I'm not angry over what happened but I am very hurt. I have served the congregation for most of my life. First as Junior Pastor under my sister, who started the church and donated the land and building to the members of the church. After she died, I have led the church for the past 15 years. I know that Lottie wasn't thinking straight when she voted. She was so in love with a new man that arrived at the church named Bob. He wanted to become a pastor, not because he believed in the church, but he was a con man and felt he could use the church to get money out of people. I tried to block him because I won't sign off on a pastor license for someone that doesn't believe or care about the church. Lottie threw herself at him. He played it for what it was worth to him. He got a roof over his head, his meals, a job at the church, and worked to get me removed from my position. Lottie was a fool when it came to men. She wanted one so bad that she would do almost anything to get one."

Bishop asked, "I heard about the meeting you set up for Lottie to see Violet and Bob together. Is that true?"

Helena took another drink and paused before answering. "Yes. I knew that if I told Lottie that Bob was dating Violet, she wouldn't believe me. I wanted her to see for herself. It was best to end the false

FLAWED DECISIONS MURDER

hopes she had of being with Bob as soon as possible. Ending any relationship hurts, but the longer it goes on, the more pain there is. I was thinking what was best for Lottie. When did this death occur? Can you tell me anything about what happened?"

Robinson said, "We can only tell you that she was found at 8:00 this morning. We are trying to determine how and why the death occurred. Can you tell us where you were from the time of 5:00 a.m. to 8:00 a.m. this morning?"

Helena laughed a little, "What makes you think my 5 foot, 110-pound, and 80-year-old body could murder a much larger person? Never mind. I was out of town. I went to see Pauline. She is the person acting as Bob's instructor for the classes to become a pastor. I told her all I knew about the church and the situation. We have known each other for 20 years. She knows how much I care about our faith. At her suggestion, at 8:00 a.m., we went to the office of the governing board. I told my story there also. Again, I am very well-known and respected. I'm sure the authority will come to the church and investigate. I expect this to all be blown over soon. I had no reason to murder Lottie for her poor decision. I have witnesses that can state that I couldn't have done it. I will be glad to give you the names and numbers to call and confirm my story."

MIA TENROC

Robinson asked, "Have you talked to your daughter, Grace? We have been looking for her to interview but she hasn't been to the church or at home all day."

Helena looked angry, "I'm sure she has nothing to add that could help. I want to be here when you interview her."

Bishop pointed out, "She is an adult so you can't be here. If you have reason to be concerned about her answers, she can have an attorney present."

Helena acted softer, "I don't fear her answers, but she isn't exactly a mature adult. That is why she lives with me and I take care of her."

Bishop pressed the point, "We have heard she didn't handle the church's funds correctly, but so far there has been no formal complaint against her. We only want to discuss the situation of Lottie."

Helena walked proudly out of the station. Bishop shared her opinion of the interview with Robinson. "I don't believe she did the murder. We will check out the story but I'm sure that is a dead end. I do believe that she is a manipulator like the others say. I believe she set Lottie up to discover the Violet relationship for selfish purposes."

Story

Chapter 52 – Grace

Grace entered the Police Station, accompanied by a very young man who carried his briefcase with pride. "I'm Mr. John Preston, esquire, and this is my client, Grace. Detectives Bishop and Robinson are requesting an interview."

The desk clerk rang Bishop's extension number with a voice that would not be overheard, "You're not going to believe these two."

The detectives smiled when they saw Grace dressed as she would have probably 40 years before. She was in a jumper, blouse with puffy sleeves, a bow at the neck, and canvas shoes. Her bleached blond hair was teased on top with a bow in the back. Her bright blue eye shadow was matching the color of her eyes. Mr. Preston was probably in his mid-twenties

MIA TENROC

but looked more like a teenager. His ill-fitting suit added to the impression of a boy trying to act like a man.

Bishop stepped forward to thank them for coming in and escorted them to an interview room. Mr. Preston asked, "I want to know if my client is a suspect for anything. It's our understanding that there has been a death. Is that true?"

Robinson replied, "Lottie Simmer's body was found at the church today. We haven't determined if it was a homicide or a suicide. Needless to say, we don't have a report from the coroner or the forensic team back yet. We are currently interviewing people acquainted with the victim, trying to find out any information that would help our investigation. Grace, I understand that you knew Lottie and even had dinner with her a couple of nights ago."

Grace looked at her attorney. He was non-committal so she assumed it was ok for her to answer. "Did you know I use to babysit Mr. Preston? He was always so smart and mature for his age. I'm not the least bit surprised at his success. Thank you for joining me today, John." Robinson cleared his throat trying to get Grace to focus on the conversation. "Oh, the question." Grace giggled.

FLAWED DECISIONS MURDER

Robinson was starting to show irritation. "This is not a joke, Miss Grace. Someone died today and I consider that serious business."

Grace giggled again so Mr. Preston explained, "This giggle is a nervous habit. I assure you that Grace is taking this interview very seriously."

Grace smiled, "I'm sorry to hear Lottie died. I have no doubt that she committed suicide. After all, did you see her? She was actually very comfortable financially, and I hear she was a good business woman, but she was so homely looking. She threw herself after every single man that came to the church. She never had a true boyfriend that I know of. She really had her eye on Bob. If it wasn't suicide, he would be my first suspect. He was playing her for her money and to get a position in the church, then he was going to dump her for Violet. I think that's why she committed suicide. It's not like Violet is such a prize catch, but to be dumped for someone so short and stocky is an insult."

Grace paused for a breath. Bishop asked, "Why do you think he was going to dump her for Violet? Was there any gossip in the church about it?"

Grace giggled, "We went out to dinner, and to our surprise, Bob was playing in a band just across the street. We decided to stop in to have drink and enjoy the music. We walked in and there he was with

260

MIA TENROC

Violet. A very unfortunate dose of reality for poor Lottie. We left right away."

Robinson asked, "I understand that Lottie was instrumental in your being fired from your position as bookkeeper at the church. What was your reaction to that?"

Preston leaned over and whispered to Grace. Grace smiled, "There's nothing to worry over." To the detectives, she explained, "Lottie was the leader in not only getting me fired but also for getting my mother, who has given her whole life to that church, demoted. If anything, I believe that is even more proof that she committed suicide. We have been so good to her. I can only imagine she was full of guilt after she had time to think about her actions."

Bishop asked, "You weren't angry with her?"

Preston tried take control of the conversation. "It looks to me like you are accusing my client of murdering this woman. I don't believe we should continue to answer your questions."

Again, his client ignored his advice, "Of course, it is very upsetting to be treated so shabbily after all my years working in the church. It's never nice to be falsely accused of wrongdoing when I haven't done anything remotely wrong. I am a spiritual person and believe that right will win over wrong. I believe that no matter how badly someone treats you, the best

261

FLAWED DECISIONS MURDER

thing to do is show kindness and compassion. I will be exonerated soon, and everything will be fine."

Preston looked relieved that Grace pulled off the rehearsed statement with such sincerity. Before they arrived, Grace was saying that Lottie got what she deserved. He had to explain to her that she needed to act more compassionate.

The questioning moved on to Bob. Grace added insight, "He's good looking enough, but to me, he comes off as a slippery-type person. He just shows up on the grounds one day, and the next thing you know, he's flirting with women. Next, he decides he has the right material to become a pastor. We are a church that communicates with spirits. I don't believe that man has the emotional quality to feel anything supernatural."

Robinson finished with a final question. "Have you ever known Lottie to drink or do drugs?"

Grace snorted, "Never. She like to be in control at all times. She was a very neat, organized, proper person, to my knowledge, of course. Suicide is control. Hanging is neat and clean."

Robinson and Bishop almost came out of their chairs with that mistake. They wanted to get all their facts in a row before making the arrest but how else would Grace know it was a hanging?

262

Abletown

Chapter 53 – Peter's Dilemma

"Those interviews in the Spirit Murders story catches you up to the point that I've told the others," Jean told Gwen.

Gwen was grateful. "That was so nice of you to take this private time with me. I was disappointed that the nurse on the next shift didn't show up and I had to do a double. I'm going to head for home to catch some sleep, so I will be fresh for tonight."

Jean observed, "You seem so much happier since you came to town. You have been a great addition to our water aerobics group."

Gwen confessed, "I was pretty miserable when I moved here. It was bad enough that my husband committed adultery, leading to my divorce, but it is

FLAWED DECISIONS MURDER

the betrayal of my children in supporting his decisions and welcoming his new bride that hurt the most. I thought I had friends but when I would call up ladies that I ran around with for years, they acted like I was poison. I guess they were afraid I would infect their marriages."

Jean smiled, "I experienced those same exact things in the past. I understand the loss."

"At least I can relate to Fannie with being alone but happy. You have Nick, which is wonderful for you, but you don't act like you have to be constantly together. You seem to have plenty of room in your life for your friends, married or not. That really is true for Josephine and Belinda as well. I don't want to seem like a gossip, but I'm not sure that I understand Eve's relationship. She's married but every night, she is out with this younger man. I like Eve a lot but I'm not comfortable with the situation."

Jean shared what she hoped was wisdom. "Nigel and Eve have too many differences to enjoy being in the same home. He is a hoarder who dislikes neatness and cleanliness. Eve can't stand his junkpiles. She went through so much stress when they lived in the city and were constantly being fined by the county for Nigel's mess in the yard. They considered moving him to the country, so that they would each have their own space, as the best solution. They are still honoring their marriage. Eve is disappointed that Nigel makes so little effort to see her. It's always her going to see him. Nick and I thought Eve would like to go riding on a real motorcycle. As for Connor, his wife couldn't handle the danger that he faced every day as a police officer and so left him recently. Connor and Eve both needs their egos boosted. They enjoy each other's company, but she is so much older than him, and he still wants to marry and have children, so this will remain as a friendship."

Gwen said quietly, "He spent the night a couple of days ago."

Jean laughed, "The whole town knows this. There is almost nothing that happens that doesn't get on the grapevine. I have no doubt that someone has told Nigel. I would say the next move is his. Eve said they had a couple of drinks when they went to dinner. They came back to the house and had a couple more. Connor felt it was best not to drive so he spent the night in the second bedroom. I believe Eve because she doesn't have the talent of telling a believable lie. Speaking of telling lies, someone is headed this way that had been greatly deceived." Daisy, Peter Crambert's wife, walked onto the porch. "Hi, Daisy, this is Gwen. She is new to town and lives on Third Street across from Josephine and Eve."

FLAWED DECISIONS MURDER

Daisy gave a polite, quick smile, "Welcome to the neighborhood. Jean, I really need to talk to you about something. I think it's really important."

Gwen excused herself, "I just worked a double shift and was headed home. Why don't you take my seat? I'm sure we will see each other around town."

Daisy was grateful that Gwen took the hint to leave since her conversation needed to be private. "Jean, everyone in town is acting like I have a disease or something. No one is taking my phone calls. I run into people I know and they make an excuse not to talk. I have had people wave and shout hi, but then cross the street rather than speak to me. Peter was supposed to be home for lunch, but it's 3:00 and he hasn't taken my calls or returned my texts. I know he is worried about something but he won't talk to me about it. What is going on?"

Jean noticed Mr. Manor's car pulling up to the curve. Peter jumped out and ran to the porch. "What are you doing talking to the enemy? Let go home, now!" He grabbed Daisy's arm and pulled her from the seat.

Daisy jerked her arm away. "I want to know why this town won't talk to me! People I have known for years won't look me in the eye. You won't tell me anything and I figure Jean is the only one in town that

266

MIA TENROC

won't lie to me. She is not our enemy! She is my friend!"

Jean spoke, "Peter, don't tell me you are going to be one of those politicians that tells their wife the bad news at the last minute, then push her out to a press conference in a state of shock to look like she is standing behind you. After over 40 years of marriage, she deserves more respect from you."

Peter turned in anger, "What are you talking about? There isn't going to be any press conference!"

Right at that moment, a truck with men drove by with the windows down. A man shouted, "Hey, Peter, do you know any other prostitutes? Did you kill her?"

Jean's eyes were on Daisy. She jumped in time to catch her body, guiding it into the chair she had just vacated, to keep her from collapsing onto the porch. With tears in her eyes, Daisy asked Peter, "What have you done? What are you doing to me?"

Jean looked at the windows of the home and spotted people looking out and no doubt listening. "This is not the place to talk. Either go to the office, home, or to my room."

Peter answered, "We will go home."

Daisy got bold, "Oh no, we aren't! I want to know the truth right now and for the first time in our marriage, I don't know if I would believe what you

FLAWED DECISIONS MURDER

say. We will go to Jean's room. I want her here to make sure I get the full story."

In the room, Jean kept quiet. This was Peter's time to do the talking. "I don't have any money saved for my retirement. I was never paid a fair wage for all the hard work I did for this town. The developers, wanting to update this old town from the dark ages, offered me a paid position if I helped them get ordinances passed that will let them build. I wouldn't have to work, except to be the liaison between the company and the town. I was doing what Jamison Bottoms, the president of the company, told me to do. He gave me money and told me to pay a consultant and a photographer. I paid them through money orders as instructed, using the money the developers donated to the campaign. I didn't realize until today that they were setting me up to make sure I did what I promised I would. If I didn't, they would've exposed me and reported me to the IRS. I never talked to the consultant nor did I know her real profession. She was murdered, but I had nothing to do with it. I repeat, I never ever saw her. As soon as I found out what was happening, I got Mr. Manor to go with me to the police so I could cooperate without getting any charges pressed against me. Before today, I had trusted the developer's attorney for any advice."

Jean now spoke, "You can tell by the shouts outside, the gossip in town has part of the information

268

MIA TENROC

correct. The town watched the news and saw the story about Missy aka Trudy Must being murdered. They saw her around town, helping on Leon's campaign. You weren't smart enough to buy the money orders out of town. It didn't take the tellers long to figure out you hired her to disrupt Leon's campaign. The town hasn't figure out that some of the money orders were for the photograph. They think you were just planning to announce that Leon lacked moral character by letting a prostitute work on his campaign. I doubt you killed her because you are left-handed. This is just my guess; Nick and I never discuss his cases."

Daisy looked up as Peter asked, "What does my being left-handed have to do with anything?"

Jean repeated, "It's just my unprofessional opinion, but when I was identifying the body, I noticed there was a bruise on the left side of her chin with a cut. It was probably delivered at the time of death. That would mean the person was right-handed."

Daisy's mouth was open. She closed it to ask, "How would you know this woman? Why would you know about the cut being at the time of death?

Jean smiled, "I worked the crime beat for a newspaper for years. The way the blood forms on a cut is different if it is after or during the time of death. I saw a woman, naked in the woods, and they wanted

FLAWED DECISIONS MURDER

to know if this was the woman I saw. I was the one that told them about her working for Leon's campaign. You can do whatever you want about this, Peter, but the people in town are questioning if you are the murderer. I think I would have that press conference and tell the whole true."

Peter asked, "You think telling the people that I made a deal to force the town out of the dark ages is good campaign strategy? I'm going home to think but I feel it best for me to keep my mouth shut. This town may gossip but they won't totally believe anything without proof."

Jean sarcastically responded, "Yeah, good idea, but do you think Leon is going to keep his mouth shut about someone being murdered that worked for him? He is going to defend himself. The election is two days from now. Tomorrow night, you have a final debate before the town, in the town square. You better decide what you are going to say."

Abletown

Chapter 54 – Following Leads

"Jean is really amazing. She should have been a police detective. When viewing Trudy's body, she picked up on all the clues and assumptions like we did," said Janice.

Nick laughed, "That's why we have a total honesty policy. I can tell what she is thinking sometimes and she can do the same with me. It took so long getting all the information from Peter, but I think we still have time to go check out the Post Office before they close."

Janice let out a woo-hoo, "I got a hit. I've been checking the incoming calls to Trudy's phone. Most are from burner phones, except a couple of girlfriends. I have one call from a man named Luis Hedd. I have an address showing that he owns a big construction

FLAWED DECISIONS MURDER

company over on 33rd Street. Looks like the man has money. There are six sets of initials in Trudy's book and LH is one of them."

The two detectives rushed to the Post Office. Nick smiled because a man he knew was behind the counter. That meant he would get more cooperation than with a stranger. "Brian, good to see you. I'm here on business. I need the information on who rents P.O. Box 137. Do you know how often he comes in?"

Brian started looking at the records immediately. "Great to see you, Nick. Always glad to help. Here is the name of the box renter, Billy Grely. You just missed him. He left about a half hour ago. Not a friendly or chatty man. He always looks slimy. We call him Grease Grely. He comes in almost every day, usually in the afternoon."

Nick thanked him and said, "We will be back tomorrow." In the car, Nick suggested to Janice. "We have time to run by this business owned by Hedd. Usually when dealing with a man with something to hide, it's best to not go to his home." They pulled up to the business and went inside. "Good afternoon. Is Mr. Hedd available?"

The receptionist, trying to look efficient, responded, "I'm not sure. He is in the office but he may be in a meeting right now. I will buzz his office to see. Whom shall I say is calling on him?" Nick

MIA TENROC

gave only their names. The girl repeated them into the phone. "I'm sorry but he said he is too busy right now to see you."

Nick and Janice pulled out their badges. "Please ask him again."

The receptionist went pale and told the person on the other end of the line, "It's the police." To Nick, she said, "He says he always has time for the police. Let me escort you back."

Janice had found the lead so Nick felt it should be her interview. "We are here because it seems you are acquainted with a woman named Trudy Must. We thought you might be willing to answer our questions here instead of at your home."

Luis gritted his teeth, "I can't say I'm surprised to see you. I do appreciate your discretion. My family is not aware of my extra activities. I didn't kill her."

Janice assured him, "We aren't accusing you of that, for now anyway. Do you want to tell us about the association or do you want a question at a time? Let's start with the fact that you appear to be one of six regulars. It doesn't appear she worked the streets, shall we say. Do you know the other men? Where did you meet up? How often did you see Trudy?"

Luis whispered, "Can we not say that name out loud, just in case someone is listening?" Janice

273

FLAWED DECISIONS MURDER

nodded yes, so Luis continued, "There are six of us that work together. I will type their names for you. We are all in the construction business, so we are good friends. We found out we all wanted just a little something more than what we got at home. Sammy is the one that had been using Trudy's services. We don't see her enough to keep her in a room. Besides, a monthly payment would be something that a private detective could easily trace if it ever came to that for any of us. We have burner phones that we used to contact her. One of us gets a hotel room for a few days each month and we take turns visiting the room. We use cash if we can, or we find some excuse for a business meeting to be held at the hotel; that way, it's a business expense write-off. The agreement was that we each give her, in cash, a monthly fee. She promised discretion and to not to be with other men. There is always the fear of surprise germs or disease not only for us but for her too. We have been in this arrangement for a few years now. It worked well. I actually liked her as a person. She wasn't cheap or vulgar. We would talk and laugh besides our time in the other position. I'm sorry this has happened to her. I really don't have much additional information. Any questions?"

"Can you tell me the businesses these men work at or own?" Janice asked.

274

MIA TENROC

Luis named the businesses associated with each man. The third down was the owner of Modern Change Builders. As much as Janice and Nick tried not to show a response, they did. Luis continued the list but then said, "That's what I was afraid of when I heard about the murder. I know how desperately he wants a foothold in the Abletown area. Am I guessing right?"

Nick responded, "I'm afraid we can't confirm or deny that. I would greatly appreciate you not telling any of the other five about our visit or you giving us the list and what we discussed."

Luis got up to shake hands with the two detectives. "I can't tell you how much I appreciate your coming here instead of my home. The last thing I want is for my friends to know I gave information, so you can count on me not to say a word. If this conversation never came out, I would be grateful. One day, I was headed to meet Trudy and was running late. I left my spare phone on my desk. That one time, I used my private phone to make the call and deleted the information immediately. Should I guess that was my downfall?"

Janice confirmed that to be true. In the car, on the way to the office, Janice said, "Not too many people are as clever as they think. The bad guy's arrogance and ignorance are how we can get our jobs done. I

275

FLAWED DECISIONS MURDER

have a gut feeling we will find the proof to connect this guy from Modern Change Builders to the murder."

Story

Chapter 55 – Getting the Facts

The minute Grace was out of the station, Bishop was on the phone with Lisette and Richard. "Did either of you tell anyone that Lottie died by hanging?"

Lisette sounded surprised, "Of course not. You told us to tell no one. I blind-copied you on the email that I sent to the church members. It says that Lottie died at the church. I explained that since it was an unexpected death, that the police were required to investigate. The message tried to sound reassuring that we expected it to be standard procedure and be over quickly, but that no one was to go to the church unless they contacted either Richard or I. It expressed that it should only be a few days before things were back to normal. I said I would send out an email either late Tuesday or on Wednesday to let them know if

FLAWED DECISIONS MURDER

service would occur. Of course, I offered to meet with or pray with anyone that was distraught over the situation. There have been no calls but I did get emails back asking if there was anything that they could do. The question came about when the funeral service would be. I did a second mass email, which included you, stating that said service couldn't be determined at this time and that I will communicate anything I hear from the police."

Richard added, "Everything Lisette said is true. She hasn't spoken to anyone. Bob called but Lisette didn't want to speak to him so I took that call. He asked when he should go to the church to clean. I told him not until we let him know. He didn't ask questions or push for information. To be honest, we are both very shaken by this and really don't want to talk to anyone right now. Do you mind if I ask why you are wondering this?"

Bishop answered, "Sorry, I can't say right now. I do appreciate you keeping everything confidential. It makes our job so much easier. I wanted to confirm one more thing. Lisette, didn't you say the alarm wasn't on when you got to the church?" Lisette confirmed that was true.

Robinson assigned an assistant to review red-light cameras from the time Violet left and Lisette

MIA TENROC

arrived. She was given the license number, and make and model of cars for Grace, Bob and Helena.

Bishop called Bob's cell number. He answered immediately, "I was wondering if you can come by the station. I wanted to confirm just two things. It won't take long."

Bob arrived in minutes. "I really cared about Lottie. She was a good friend to me when I needed one the most. She took me in and gave me employment. What can I do to help?"

Robinson asked, "You said when you were leaving that you had set the alarm. The code had been changed. Did Lottie give you the new code number?" Bob confirmed it was true. "Lottie never did drugs or drink enough to lose control. Violet said she turned down the opportunity to use the peyote but then said later that Lottie seem high. Did you give her the drug?"

Bob looked like a deer in headlights. He thought before answering. He decided the truth was the best thing he could do. He wasn't guilty of anything else. "Yes. I'm being honest so you have no reason to suspect me. No one at church knew the truth about my son choosing to leave me. I was hurt that he didn't appreciate what a good dad I was all those years. I didn't want her to tell anyone. Lottie had a high-level government job. I thought if I had something on her,

FLAWED DECISIONS MURDER

because doing drugs would get her fired, then maybe we could make a pact never to tell on each other. I know that was a dirty thing to do. I regret it now but I didn't know what to do at the time and now know I would never use it against her. I put peyote powder in the creamer and then when she got coffee, I knew she would include cream and sugar. I flushed the remaining cream down the toilet before I left." Bob left the station after being told to not leave town nor to tell anyone what he did. He assured them that neither he nor Violet talked to anyone about the event.

The next step for the detectives was to interview the alarm system company. After introductions were made, the questioning began. "How does the alarm system work? Is there a way for someone to get into the church if they didn't have the code?"

Mr. Jones said he didn't want to answer because of his customer's confidentiality agreement. After being served with a warrant, he asked, "If I cooperate, can you keep it a secret?"

Robinson said, "If we can, we will, but I can't guarantee that promise. Either you cooperate or we will get an order to seize your companies' computers and halt your business while we find out for ourselves."

"Alright. I didn't think you would be understanding. You enter a code to deactivate the

MIA TENROC

alarm when you first enter the church and the last person enters the same code to reactivate the alarm when they leave. I have no clue how many people have the code because they can give it to anyone they want. Everyone uses the same code." As he spoke, Mr. Jones was searching on his computer. "It looks like the code was changed on Sunday afternoon, about 2:30 p.m. on the church computer. You can change the code either from the computer at the church or the one that Pastor Helena has. It looks like on Monday morning, around 6:00 a.m., the computer Helena has entered into the system. Just in case there is some weird glitch in the system, there is a way to bypass entering the current code. To do that, Helena created a secret set of questions that only she would know. Those questions were answered and the code was reset to the one that was previously used prior to the change on Sunday afternoon. It was definitely done from Pastor Helena's computer."

The detective got Mr. Jones to sign a statement and give any screen prints he could to show the transactions.

The final piece of the puzzle came in with the evidence on the rope and robe that was on the victim. There was DNA of both Lottie and Grace. Lottie's was only around the noose area whereas Grace's was both on the noose and the part of the rope tied to the railing on the wall. Both of their DNA was on the

FLAWED DECISIONS MURDER

ladder. This case had an easy solution. There was enough evidence to convict Grace.

The final piece came from the red-light cameras, showing Grace had left her home and drove in the direction of the church at the right time.

Story

Chapter 56 – Caught

Bishop and Robinson was at the door of the house where Grace lived with her mother, armed with warrants. Twenty-four hours after the murder was discovered, they had their answers. They rang the bell and Grace answered. Bishop began reading the Miranda Rights.

Helena ran into the room, "What is going on here? What are you doing?"

Robinson explained, "We are arresting your daughter for the murder of Lottie Simmer."

Helena turned to her daughter, "Don't say a word until I arrive with an attorney. Remember, not a single word." She turned to the officers, "You are so wrong

FLAWED DECISIONS MURDER

on this! My daughter would never hurt anyone! I will sue the department and both of you individually!"

Bishop handed another warrant to Helena, "This gives us a right to take all the electronics in the house and to search for any other clues."

Experienced officers of the law know it doesn't do any good to argue or explain themselves in spite of the threats. They calmly went about their business.

At the station, a much more experienced and mature attorney arrived with Helena to see Grace. Grace said, "No mother, I haven't said a word. They did ask some questions and I just sat and stared at them. Lottie committed suicide. I have it on my phone."

Helena looked shocked. She was having trouble breathing. "What are you talking about? You told me that you weren't at to the church that morning."

Grace giggled, "I know it was wrong to lie. I went over and watched her put the noose around her neck and jump."

Helena was leaning in so they could whisper, "Did she say anything like 'I want to kill myself'?"

Grace laughed, "No, she thought she was going to fly."

MIA TENROC

The attorney, Mr. Peterson, interrupted, "I think it is best that Grace continues not to say a word. As her representative, they have to share the evidence with me. We will see how the case stands after that."

As soon as permitted, the district attorney and the two detectives had their meeting with Mr. Peterson. Helena insisted on attending. "This rope has Grace's DNA on it."

Helena jumped in, "I know it has Bob's DNA. He touched it at the festival we had recently."

They answered, "Yes, it did have Bob and other people's DNA on it, but his was spread throughout the rope. You can tell by the spacing that he was winding it up. Grace's DNA is only at the ends. The one end was tied to the wall and the other end was the noose and where it was place through the robe. And before you ask, yes, Bob's DNA was on the robe but not at the neckline, where Grace's DNA was around the collar."

"What other evidence do you have?" asked Mr. Peterson.

Bishop's answer was surprising, "Here on Helena's computer is where she used the secret password to bypass the alarm and reset it to the previous passcode. There was no one else home at the time and only Helena and Grace even knew that it could be done. Here is Grace's phone where she taped

FLAWED DECISIONS MURDER

the murder. Yes, Lottie climbed the ladder and put the noose on her neck, but as you can see in the video, Lottie was not in a state of mind that could comprehend what was going on. This is murder in the 1st degree. Here let me play it for you."

She pressed play on the video on her phone. You could hear Grace saying, "What are you doing, Lottie? You saw me jump from the ladder and fly to the ground. Are you wanting to fly, too, Lottie? Wow! That was a big flight. Do you want to do it again? Are you going to put on the robe with big wing-like sleeves? Fly, Lottie! Fly!" Then was the sound of Grace laughing.

Later, Mr. Peterson talked with Helena and Grace in private. He explained, "There is no overcoming the evidence. I believe we need to get a professional to determine that Grace isn't mentally responsible for her actions. There is no way to win an acquittal."

Grace still insisted, "She did it to herself."

Story

Chapter 57 – Goodbye

Lisette delivered the news from the alter of the church the following Sunday, "Lottie Simmer died on Monday. We need to pray for her spirit. Grace has plead not guilty by reason of insanity, even though she still doesn't believe she did anything wrong. She will be sent to a mental hospital for those that have committed serious crimes but will be receiving treatment for her thought process. Helena has volunteered to start a church at that facility This church has been hit with much sadness and negative experiences. I do believe we can recover. We need to learn and grow."

After everyone else had left, Lisette went to sit in her office. Bob came in and tried to go around the desk to give her a hug. Lisette pointed to the chair on

FLAWED DECISIONS MURDER

the other side of the desk before he could reach her. "Sit. We need to talk. I know about your lies. I know that your son left you and that he is healthy. Why would you lie to me like that?"

Bob was taken by surprise. "Where did you get that idea?"

Lisette was angry, "No more lies! Your son talked to Lottie. She called and repeated what happen to Richard. Yes, I'm getting it third-hand but I believe it to be true. Why did you lie? No one here even knew you had a son. There was no need to tell a fake story."

Bob realized that he was caught and told the truth, "My son left the night before I met you. I got drunk. I just woke up to let the dog out. It ran away and I was trying to catch it. I guess I was still upset that my son left me after I spent all those years loving him and raising him. You are such an understanding person that felt I could talk to you. You would have thought I was a horrible person if I told you the whole truth so I was telling a half-truth, half-lie story. The lies seem to take over the truth."

Lisette already had her mind made up but wanted to give Bob a chance to change it. "I can't recommend you to be a pastor if you lie every time it suits you. The fact that you lied to me so much makes me uncomfortable that you are even here. I'm terminating your employment with the church and I ask you never to return. I don't know if all this would have happened at the church if it wasn't led by your design. I feel, in a sense, that you are responsible for Lottie's death. No one can look at you and not see how you used Lottie. This church can't heal with your presence. I hope you understand that."

Bob was actually agreeing with the assessment of the situation. "I understand. I will move on. Grey and Violet want to return to his home for his final days. I want to go with them, so it all works out for the best."

Violet had been standing outside the door. Lisette was worried about Bob's reaction to her decision to let him go from the church. She didn't want to ask Richard to be there because his feelings towards Bob had reached the point of hatred. Violet was now the head chair of the board, replacing Lottie, so Lisette felt she was the one that should be there. Due to Bob being such a physically strong man, Violet asked Lonny to be there just in case. The two moved away when Bob got up to leave.

That evening, Lonny called Bob, "So we got good news and bad news. Our original guitar player has totally recovered and wants his position back in the band. We have been together for years and there is no way I can say no. Look, Bob, you have so much talent, you shouldn't be doing local gigs. Why don't you head to Nashville? You could make the big time."

FLAWED DECISIONS MURDER

Bob accepted this gracefully as well, "I knew this was temporary to begin with. I think it's good timing. I plan to leave town anyway. Thanks for letting me sit in. Good luck with the band."

Bob took all his belongings from Lottie's house, and turned the keys over to the Personal Representative of her estate. He headed for Violet's house. Bob really did love Violet. There was no one home when he arrived. Bob tried to call but there was no answer. Violet texted Bob back, "Look under the mat."

There was a letter for him. It read, "Bob, my father and I left for his home hours ago. This is a family moment, and even though we enjoy each other's company, you are not family. I have many relatives that will support me through this difficult time. I will be staying there and running the family business. My store manager is capable of running my store there. I don't know that I love you enough to marry you. Enjoying one's company isn't the same as the commitment to marriage. I'm sorry but this is goodbye."

Bob was a little sad but then realized, "It's time to move on. New adventures await me and Violet would never understand my desire for the fame that will come my way in Nashville. This really is goodbye."

Abletown

Chapter 58 – Murder Solved

While Jean was explaining the solution to the murder from long ago, Nick was working on the solution of the murder of Trudy Must. Janice was working behind the counter of the post office. Nick was sitting in the back room visiting with his friend, Brian. "I hope this arrest doesn't create too much excitement for our customers."

Nick smiled, "It can't be helped. It appears that the address on your records for Mr. Grely isn't current. It was a rundown apartment complex and he is no longer a resident there."

Janice came to the door, "Now!"

Nick and Janice approached Mr. Grely. He was looking at his mail and didn't realize they were

FLAWED DECISIONS MURDER

headed towards him until they spoke, "Mr. Grely, we are taking you in for questioning for the death of Trudy Must aka Missy."

Mr. Grely didn't look shocked or worried, "I want to call my lawyer."

At the station, Mr. Grely was given his one call. It wasn't to a law firm but to the offices of Modern Change Builders. "You need to send your attorney over right away."

A man was talking on the other end of the line, "You were hired to take pictures, not to commit murder. Our attorney will not be representing you on that matter. We have to protect the name of our company so don't call here again."

Billy Grely turned to Nick and said, "I need a court-appointed attorney for now."

Again, the DNA evidence was the matter that won the case. The ring that Mr. Grely wore was shaped like a dragon. There was a very little bit of Trudy's DNA on the ring. Nick questioned Mr. Grely, "You committed murder. The question is what level: 1st degree premediated, 2nd degree in the heat of the moment, or manslaughter, accidental without intent?"

Grely's court-appointed attorney, Willie Clemon, did the best job he could with working with the DA. Jean could identify the odd hair-growth pattern and

MIA TENROC

birth mark on the back of Billy's neck as being with Trudy on the date and time in question. The DNA evidence on the ring proved that he punched Trudy. Grely was willing to accept a 5-year manslaughter charge in exchange for a confession and giving evidence about the owner of Modern Change Builder doing illegal campaign contributions and organizing the events they hoped would discredit Leon Pierre's campaign.

Mr. Grely said, "Trudy, or Missy, which was the name I knew her by, was a stupid girl. Four times, she told me that she was sure that Mr. Pierre accepted her advances. She did warn that he was a proper person and even if he did respond to her, it would be a one-time thing. I got sick of her calling me out and nothing happening. She was wasting my time. I found out about the six rich men she was sleeping with on a regular basis. I tried to tell her that eventually they would dump her for a younger woman. After all, Missy was in her late 30's. I offered to take pictures of them together so that the day they dumped her, she could request they continue making payments to her. She was too stupid to see what I offered was a benefit to her in the future. Blackmail may be illegal but it's not like what those men were doing was right. Missy threatened to tell the men about my offer. She told me that I was getting well-paid for getting the pictures of her and Leon. We were shouting at each other and she

FLAWED DECISIONS MURDER

pushed me. I punched her only one time. It was self-defense, to keep her from pushing or punching me again. Missy's fell back and her head hit a tree stump. I didn't mean to kill her. It was an accident."

Nick relayed the story to Jean that afternoon, "We might not have solved this one without your help. Thank you for being so smart and observant. What has been happening in town with the candidates?"

Jean suggested, "They are supposed to do a final debate tonight because voting is tomorrow morning. Why don't we go down to see what they have to say?"

All the friends except Priscilla sat together on lawn-chairs as Mr. Pierre stood on the courthouse steps ready for their last debate. Mr. Cranbert was not there.

Mr. Pierre began at the appointed time. "I don't know where Mr. Cranbert is but he has good reason to hide. I'm not going to go on about the illegal and immoral judgment he used in hiring someone to make advances towards me and a photographer to capture the picture to discredit me. I was mayor of a much larger city for years. I have a solid record to run on of doing what I promise. The main reason I entered this race was to protect his town from overdevelopment. I have always been charmed by Abletown's beauty and friendliness. This is a town of good values and I plan

294

MIA TENROC

to do all I can to continue to keep Abletown the stellar city it has always been. I will protect the downtown area. I will make sure that crime is kept out of this city. I will be willing to listen to the majority of the residents and do the will of the people if you elect me mayor of this great town. I didn't accept money for my campaign. I paid for the cost myself so I'm not obligated to anyone. I didn't accept the advances of any woman. I love my wife and family and there is no one that could come between us. I hope I have your vote tomorrow. Thank you for your time."

It was time for Mr. Cranbert to speak but instead of him doing so, Priscilla climbed the steps. "Peter Crambert can't be here tonight. He isn't feeling well." There were many comments from the crowd that Priscilla ignored. "Peter realizes he may have made a couple of bad decisions. He has been your mayor for 20 years. He has always done right for us in the past and I believe we can trust him to do so in the future. It would be wrong of us to turn our backs on this town's leader for someone that moved here less than a year ago. Mr. Pierre isn't one of us. Vote for Peter and keep this town in the hands of our own."

Abletown

Chapter 59 – The Vote

The town may not have had a verbal response to Priscilla's words but the ballot box did the talking for the town. "As head of the election committee, I announce the winner of the Mayor race for the town of Abletown. The winner is Belinda."

Belinda was shocked and shouted, "I wasn't running."

"Do you decline the nomination?"

Leon Pierre came over to Belinda, "Please accept it. You are the person that this town listens to and trusts. I believe you are the person this town needs. When you were out campaigning for me, people could see your wisdom and judgment. I request, on behalf of myself and the town, for you to please accept."

MIA TENROC

Belinda looked worried, "I've never been a mayor before. I will need the help and support of everyone here if I accept the position."

There was a very loud cheer from all those gathered outside the courthouse steps.

Priscilla had been standing across the street from the crowd. She left and headed to Mr. Manor's office. "I can't believe those people. Belinda didn't even want the job and here they go and vote for her instead of the man that served them all those years."

Mr. Manor studied Priscilla, "Yes, Peter did serve this town for a long time, but his judgment at the end wasn't the best for anyone. Why are you so stuck on being on his side after it is now known what he did?"

Priscilla stubbornly continued, "He is my Mayor. You don't turn your back on someone just because he supposedly did those things. I don't have proof that he hired the woman and photographer."

"You mean him confessing to it isn't proof enough for you? Priscilla, you do realize that Peter only got two votes. One was his own and I'm assuming the other was you. Even his wife and children admitted they wanted him to get out of the public eye. They feel their lives are ruined by his actions. Most of the people were at the diner last night. We also talked on the courthouse lawn. We asked ourselves: who could we trust? Who had the

297

FLAWED DECISIONS MURDER

best interests of the town in their heart? Everyone gave the same answer: Belinda. That is when we did the write-in campaign. I admit to being involved. I believe Belinda is such a smart person with many life experiences and that she will do a good job."

Priscilla looked crushed, "You are Peter's attorney and yet you didn't support him? You know, I'm realizing that I don't want to be a part of this town any longer. You worked against Peter. I can't get rid of those on the Trust board so I can do what I think is best for this town. My grandchildren are wealthy now due to inheritance. I think instead of giving myself to this town, I want to spend my time with them. I resign as Trustee and will have my personal items moved from the Reid mansion by the end of today."

If Priscilla hoped for a request to stay, she didn't get it. Mr. Manor calmly stated "I think that is a wise decision. I wish you all the best."

Priscillas asked, "Who is going to do all the good works I'm currently doing for the Trust?"

Mr. Manor explained, "The Board of Directors will vote on the new Trustee as it states in the Trust."

Mr. Manor was relieved that Priscilla chose to leave on her own. He was considering a vote of no-confidence for the next board meeting. Instead, there was an emergency meeting that evening.

298

MIA TENROC

Jean announced, "I'm nominating Fannie to be the successor trustee. She worked with people in nursing homes for years, so she can handle about anyone. She is very outgoing. Fannie already is doing the delivery of welcoming packages to new residents. Besides, Fannie, you have been complaining a lot about how much working at the store is hurting your back. You're always moving, lifting, and having long hours. I think you should take the job."

Everyone in the room agreed that they had total confidence in Fannie to do the job.

Fannie admitted, "Everything you said is true. While I do consider the store a success, I'm not earning as much money a year as the Trustee position will pay. I accept the position."

There was a cheer in the room. Jean said, "I can't believe what happened in our friendship with Priscilla. While everyone is entitled to their opinion, she made up the truth and believed her own false reality, even after Peter confessed. I'm glad she decided to move on and wish her well."

The meeting was adjourned and everyone headed home. Someone stepped from the shadows to speak to Jean. It was Nigel. "Jean, I hear rumors that Eve is having an affair. Is that true?"

Jean was offended to be put in the middle of the problem. "Nigel, Eve said that there is nothing

FLAWED DECISIONS MURDER

romantic between her and Connor. I believe her because Eve doesn't lie. Eve is in need of someone that will listen to her. She wants someone that wants to be with her. You prefer to live with the junk on the farm. The separate living situation is a good solution, but when do you ever call her to say thank you for paying for your lifestyle? Do you ever call her just to even say you love her? A woman needs more than what you are offering. I think her choice of having fun with Connor is safe because he is much younger and wants a family, something Eve can't provide. If you want to save you marriage, I think you need to make some effort in the relationship."

Nigel thanked her. "I'm going to Eve's house to profess my love now!"

Mia Tenroc

About the Author

Mia Tenroc started reading mysteries when she was 12 years old, Rex Stout and Agatha Christie being her favorites. She and her sister vowed to become mystery writers. Unable to work together, Mia designed the series with central characters that introduce each story in the first chapter but then each book is its own story. That way, she and her sister could write their own stories yet use these characters as the connection.

Mia's books are dedicated to demonstrating how what we say to one another really matters. She hopes to show that kind words build self-esteem and elevates people. A dedicated people watcher, Mia observes families interacting with each other which she uses as the basis for her books.

Mia tries to incorporate her small town into the books because there is a great joy in knowing your neighbors and being surrounded by family and friends. Mia loves to travel and experience the fun of seeing new place.

Made in the USA
Middletown, DE
01 December 2021